THE FIRST AMERICAN POPE

THE FIRST AMERICAN POPE

SECOND EDITION

DONALD A MICHAUD

TATE PUBLISHING
AND ENTERPRISES, LLC

Published by Tate Publishing & Enterprises, LLC
127 E. Trade Center Terrace | Mustang, Oklahoma 73064 USA
1.888.361.9473 | www.tatepublishing.com

Tate Publishing is committed to excellence in the publishing industry. The company reflects the philosophy established by the founders, based on Psalm 68:11,
"The Lord gave the word and great was the company of those who published it."

Published in the United States of America

ISBN: 978-1-63449-455-7
1. FICTION / Christian / General
2. FICTION / Christian / Futuristic
14.09.02

The first edition of The First American Pope was published on June 18, 2013 just as Pope Francis was to become the current pope. He has been a breath of fresh air in the Catholic Church. Admired by both Catholics and non-Catholics worldwide. Some of his comments and actions during his first year as Pope seems to follow many of the attributes and actions described in this novel. I personally am very pleased with his actions including his latest statements on priest celibacy. May we all pray for his continued health and wellbeing in becoming a true inclusive church leader for the entire world of believers.

Don Michaud

ACKNOWLEDGMENT

I wish to thank my brother Ron, for his editorial prowess and constructive recommendations in helping me to complete this novel.

INDEX

CHAPTER 1

THE REVELATION

As the College of Cardinals is locked in the Sistine Chapel, after three intense days of deliberation, we find Cardinal John Meyer in quiet contemplative prayer, when he hears his name called. "Cardinal John Meyer…" "Yes!" As he slowly raises his head and opens his eyes, yet not noticing anyone speaking closed to him, except he notices that all the other Cardinals in the Chapel seemed to be motionless. How could this be? As he gazed among his peers, he notices a white robed individual walking toward him.

"Who are you sir, surely you are not a Cardinal, and how can it be that you are in this locked Chapel?" 'Oh but John, don't you recall Pentecost, when I appeared to your predecessors in the locked upper room.' "But…but you can't be?" 'Oh and why not, John?' "But, you're to appear in majesty at the end of times." 'Well John, that's not for some time!'

'Thank you, John, for your prayer of concern on who is to be elected as a new Pontiff in these times of great strife, wars and imaginable environmental catastrophes. But, I have seen your great wisdom, and faith, and have come to ask you, John, to accept this new challenge to redirect my church. But you must also understand John that this will not be without personal and physical risks to you. For the Devil and his consorts, including the Illuminati and others will be there at every opportunity to try to stop you and the people you will rely on to make this request possible. There will be fatalities, but not your own; my legions of Angels will be forever at your side protecting you, until I call you to your heavenly reward'. "But Jesus, how can I ask people to put their lives in danger?" 'Like all good soldiers who believe in me, they will gladly give their lives, like the martyrs before us.'

Upon hearing this request, John, falls to his knees, and pronounces, "My Lord Jesus, I am but a humble servant. How, can I possibly be able to fulfill such a challenge?" 'Oh, you can and must, John, but I need you to be my representative Shepherd for my flock. I will be there for you, whenever you ask. John, will you take up my Cross?' "Yes Lord, if it is your will."

'John be not frightened by the events that will soon occur, for My Church needs to change dramatically if it's to enter the final era of my reign. It has to become an inclusive Universal Church for all who believe, not an exclusive one as it has become. You will be instrumental in continuing John XXIII's ecumenical vision to bringing all believers into union. I will announce you as my chosen Pope, so all will know whom to trust. But from then on, you will be the only one to see me when I appear so that we can converse in privacy.'

'It will fall on you to dramatically change the College of Cardinals after your election, for many of your fellow Cardinals, their death is near. You will promulgate the message that woman will be ordained into the priesthood for the first time, and allowed to be ordained as bishops and later elected into the College of Cardinals. Some of the women and clergy are to come into the episcopacy from ordained ministers of other churches that acknowledge the Primacy of Peter. You will be scorned and defiled for your actions, but know that you will be doing my work, and that of Our Father's.'

'Upon your election, instead of going to the balcony, as has been the custom for new pontiffs, please put on the habit of a simple monk, and walk out secretly into the plaza among the people. For it is to be among the people that you will be known.' "When the other cardinals awake they will be asked to cast their ballots without further discussions and the election will be concluded."

CHAPTER 2

A NEW POPE IS CHOSEN

Just as quickly as Cardinal Meyer saw the appearance of Jesus, He soon disappeared, and then he notice the other Cardinals started to rustle in their seats. The Dean of Cardinal raps the mallet on the desk and calls out to the Cardinal Secretary to pass out the ballots, with no further discussions by the prelates, and to vote in silence.

Each Cardinal then puts their ballots in the Holy Chalice. Upon concluding the counting, the Cardinal Secretary brings forth to the Dean of Cardinals the result of the ballot.
The Dean of Cardinals, arises in awe, "My dear Cardinals, it has been an unprecedented election, that we have a unanimous decision after such acrimonious deliberations. Will, you Cardinal John Meyer accept the honor of being our next Pope. " As the Cardinal rises, he answers 'Yes, I will accept to be your Humble Servant, Lord Jesus Christ, Lord and Savior, and GOD our Father.' At which all applaud with great spirit and admiration.

After which, the Cardinal Secretary, burns the ballots in the stove in the corner of the Chapel, so that white smoke appears for the entire world to know that a new Pope has been elected.
The Dean of Cardinal then asks Cardinal John Meyer, "By which name will you be known?", "I wish to be known as John", answered Cardinal John Meyer. The Dean of Cardinals then escorts him to the sacristy reserved for the vesting of the new Pope.

As the last Pope to bear the name of John was John XXIII, the new Pope will be recognized as Pope John XXIV. The new Pope is escorted into a room where three sets of vestments are laid out to accommodate the potential stature of any elected Holy Father. John asks all but the servant to leave the chamber. And then he asks the servant to please bring him immediately a habit of a monk. The servant a bit perplex, responds yes to the Holy Father before leaving the room. After a few minutes the servant brings him the monk's habit, upon which the new Pope then asks the servant to please remain with him, and seeks assurance of his confidence in what they will be doing.

After Pope John XXIV changes, he asks the servant to please guide him through the buildings to gain access to the plaza below. So with haste, they meander through quietly with the Pope's head covered in the monk's habit without being interrogated all the way to the middle of the Plaza.

As the new Pope arrives in the midst of St. Peter's Square, everyone starts to glance at the heavens, as the sun suddenly glows with a brilliant pulsating light in the eastern sky, the crowd becomes frightened and scared, some crying out loud as to what is possibly happening. With great amazement, they notice that the moon is now also appearing in the west with a glowing white surface. Then all of a sudden, the skies turn dark and a bedazzling display of seemingly thousands of lightning strikes and thunder are witnessed throughout the sky. Almost as quickly as it started, the sky becomes quiet with a dark blue background with all the stars in the heavens sparkling in brilliance.

Suddenly a vision appears in the middle of the skies with the appearance of two individuals and a dove, reflected on both surfaces of the sun and moon. The figure on the right is then heard to speak.

"Peace, be with you all, for I have returned to call upon all who believe in ME to come and join together in union as members of my living church. For all who believe in ME, sees the Father in ME, and I in the Father and Holy Spirit. I am calling for a union of all believers into one universal Catholic Church."

"When I came as your Messiah here on Earth, I was not here to change the cultural and historical traditions of the Jews and Gentiles that I and my apostles encountered in our time on earth. I was here to fulfill God's promise to open up the gates of heaven that had been closed because of the sin of Adam and Eve. As a baby born into a Jewish family, I was raised according to the cultural and historical customs of the time similar to the traditions and cultural customs of other nations and as similar to the Muslims or orthodox believers of today. These were very male dominated societies, whose traditions excluded females from religion and positions of authority within their culture and education. Other cultures observed these traditions on the basis of classes within their societies."

"I, the disciples, and the Prophets had to convince people that I was the Messiah as promised to your forefathers. In order for Me to be accepted as the Messiah, I had to follow the Jewish practices, customs, and religious beliefs at that time."

"My ministry was to educate My followers about a new kingdom that was not here on the earth. The early Catholic Church therefore had to speak so that the early Christians according to their cultural and historical significance traditions would understand what was being conveyed to them. Otherwise they would not have understood or been inspired to believe in Me or My teachings."

"Male dominance in the Catholic Church has been derived essentially because at the time of My ministry, the world was a male dominated society in family and government. Thus only males were allowed to be educated, vote and allowed to own property. I was born into that society, and thus the church became a male society. If I had been born today, the church episcopacy would have been very different including the male dominated church doctrines and governance."

"Those who would use the bible as their reason for exclusion of women priests are basing their premises on cultural and historical traditions and not that of My desires.

For centuries, I have used our Mother, Mary, in numerous miraculous apparitions throughout the world to advance My ministry and the acknowledgment of Our Divine Mercy in proclaiming the good news of the existence of our Father, God and the Holy Spirit."

"In addition, I have revealed myself through the lives of many of the Saints of the church, and those bearing the stigmata of My

Crucifixion, like St Francis and Padre Pio, including most recently Catalina Rivas, a housewife from Cochabamba, Bolivia, who has received messages from Mary and Me since 1993. Those events throughout the world, and even today, show that I am here with you and to continue efforts to teach you about Our divine love and mercy. Those who only would believe what the bible teaches and not recognize the interactions of Mary and Myself in the world today, have not opened their hearts to allow for divine interventions to broaden their enlightenment of God's glorious plan."

"In Matthew 19:12; It states, "There are eunuchs who were born that way from their mother's womb; and there are eunuchs who were made eunuchs by men; and there are also eunuchs who made themselves eunuchs for the sake of the kingdom of heaven. He who is able to accept this let him accept it."[1]

"This discussion of eunuchs was in the context of the question asked of Myself about whether it is good to marry. For centuries people who condemned homosexuals and lesbians were and are of the opinion that it is a "choice". I say they were born that way. Why do people condemn them? In God's eyes they are blessed, just like every other human deserving every blessing and everlasting life in the kingdom of heaven. It is MY will."

"Therefore we cannot discriminate against anyone as to which sacraments of the Church they are entitled to receive, including matrimony and holy orders. The only criteria by which we can deny anyone from receiving sacraments other than the sacrament of reconciliation and baptism are whether they are in the proper state of grace."

"Today, those orthodox traditions, customs, beliefs, prejudices, sexism, will not be allowed in a Universal Catholic Church for all believers. It is to be a church of inclusion and not exclusion just as My heavenly kingdom is. I honor My Mother, the Blessed Immaculate Mary as part of My ministry within My church, and therefore women, gays or lesbians are to become members of the church's episcopacy. They will no longer be excluded from being priest in the church or its ruling hierarchy. The College of Cardinals will have an equal number of female members, including members to be drawn from the Christian, Jewish, Protestant, and other denominations that will be joining the Universal Catholic Church. Christian, Jewish, Protestant, and other major faith denominations who want to be included in the Universal Catholic Church, are to submit names of members to be considered as their church representatives for voting positions within the Catholic Episcopacy."

"Many Christian believers of other denominations because of the differences with the Catholic Bible do not believe in certain Catholic beliefs, particularly the existence of purgatory or the devotion accorded the Blessed Mother. Because the word "purgatory" did not exist at the time of the Old Testament does not mean it does not exist, as some believe. They believed that prior to My dying on the Cross that all unclean souls went into hell until the last judgment.

Those who do not believe in purgatory, have the misconceived notion that when I died all existing sins and future sins were forgiven; therefore since they had accepted the Lord as their Savior they would go directly to heaven upon their death."

"As your souls depart from human bodies, they return to God for their Judgment. If you're soul is not pure, then it is to be purified in Purgatory for a time, not damned for eternity. Once purified, the soul is united in glory with our Heavenly Family. If your soul is in perfect grace, then you shall enter into Heaven for eternity. Never to be judged again, for there is no need for a final judgment. Please pray and do acts of penitence for the souls in purgatory. Your Heavenly Mother has asked this, so that they receive divine mercy and a shortened time in purgatory. Those in purgatory share life among you seeking to redeem their souls by putting in practice their faith works, which they did not do when they were living. Once their souls have gained perfect grace, they will receive their final judgment by being accepted by Me and welcomed by God our Father with choirs of angels and greeted by your families upon entering Heaven. They will not have to wait until the final days as had been proclaimed by others."

"As I was dying on the Cross, I turned to the thief, and said to him, "that because of your faith, you will be with Me in Heaven this day". The spilling of My blood not only saved the thief, but also released all the souls of the departed up to that time, for the Gates of Heaven had been shuttered. For those faithful souls who had been glorified that day, they entered to their Heavenly reward never to be judged again."

At that moment, the image of the Crucifixion appears in the heavens as at the moment of Jesus's death on the cross. Darkness covers the earth, suddenly multiple explosions of lightning strikes and thunder roars in every direction. Above the crucified image, a brilliant light appears as a large diamond cascading with lights emitted in all directions. A voice is heard from the Heavens, "Just as promised at My Son's death, the Gates of Heaven were then opened. At that time, you could have seen rising from the earth worldwide, the sparkle of flames emitting their lights as millions of souls ascended to Heaven." As quickly as this image of brilliant lights appeared it dissipated, and the image of Jesus reflected in the sun and the moon remained.

"The image you now see, my brothers and sisters, occurred when the Gates of Heaven received the souls that had been in limbo, as promised by My Father, at the moment of My earthly death."

"I am today, calling forth among you, My faithful servant, a new Pope, who will lead My church from this time on until he is called for his heavenly reward. I ask all of you to abide by his doctrines and changes to the church in order to reawaken the church with a new vision that includes everyone."

As the Lord hands seem to rise, suddenly the new Pope dressed in a simple monk's habit is elevated above the crowds of Saint Peter plaza. "THIS IS YOUR NEW POPE, JOHN, WHO HAS MY FAVOR, LISTEN TO HIM FOR HE HAS BEEN SANTIFIED BY ME TO LEAD MY UNIVERSAL CATHOLIC CHURCH HERE ON EARTH INTO A NEW AGE"

Just as quickly as the spectacular images in the heavens, started, they passed and the heavens returned to a pleasant sunny sky, without a cloud in the sky.

As the new Pope elevated above the crowd gently descended to the plaza surface, the throngs of faithful quickly, quietly and piously knelt around the Pope. The Pope now blessing the crowds quietly moves toward the main doors of St Peter's Basilica. The Pope's guards quickly move to the Pope's side, guiding his entrance through the crowds. The Dean of Cardinal's and the rest of the Cardinals are all in a fluster as to what has happen and what to do next.

The new Pope as he meets the group of Cardinals at the entrance tells them that he will now go to the balcony (the loggia) to speak to the faithful. He now moves on to the balcony (the loggia) still wearing the monk's habit. (The loggia is the Italian word for the actual balcony at the center of the façade of St. Peter's Basilica)

The central balcony doors of St. Peter's Basilica open, and as the crowds below see him, everyone erupts in cheers.

After a few minutes, as he waits for the crowds' cheers to subside, He lifts his hands to signal to please allow him to speak to them.

"My dear beloved brothers and sisters, we have truly witnessed a profound miracle in seeing the appearance of the Trinity, Our Lord Jesus Christ, God our Father, and Holy Spirit, to usher in a new Christian era for the world to know the Power and Glory of God, and his blessings for us all to come together as one holy and united Catholic church of believers.

I will call for a new ecumenical conclave to meet next year in Rome, and to initiate a dialogue with all our Christian, Protestant, and Jewish faiths to come and consider ways by which we can all be united as one. This will be a major challenge for us all, but come with an open heart and mind to look, listen, and contemplate in prayer what we are asked to accomplish, and not to come with a predetermined mindset, that we will never unite. Please open a dialogue with your faith brethren of what this can mean to the entire world. What an opportunity we have to break down barriers and to truly become brothers and sisters in Christ. The Lord Jesus Christ has challenged us to seek a true path to His heavenly kingdom, for which I beseech every Christian and Protestant church of every denomination to discern what the Lord Jesus Christ is asking of us. We are to open our hearts and minds to a solemn unification of our common faiths into ONE UNIVERSAL CATHOLIC CHURCH. Be it known that evil powers and doers will seek to destroy this endeavor. But if you believe, let it be done as the Lord Jesus Christ is asking of us, and the whole world will come to know peace in this new age.

Pray that we can all be accepting of the task before us to achieve what Christ Our Lord Jesus is asking us to achieve for a truly Universal Catholic Church. I will not be silent about the injustices done upon the people of the world, and I will seek to bring forth peace and tranquility that all may exist with freedom, with human rights, without hunger, free of disease, and fear of oppression.

Security, especially financial security is an important concern in many homes, businesses, nations, and churches as well. It is vital to feel safe and secure, but it is not our primary concern as followers of Christ. As Jesus instructed his disciples, mission comes first, the work of the Father, making the good news of salvation known to the world. In everything we do, let us ask how we can witness to the Gospel in deed as well as in word. How can we live a lifestyle that reflects Gospel values, in our private lives as well as in the lives as Christian communities? That is not any easy task, since we live in a world of distractions, which draws our attention away from "mission" and towards other things. Another challenge, one which all of us face daily, at home, work, school, in the marketplace, involves dealing respectfully, lovingly, and honestly with those who disagree with us, and especially those who, including ourselves, refuse to listen to another point of view.

Conflicting viewpoints can be a source of rage and hatred, even when buried from view. Each of us knows moments of private anger. We feel them in our hearts. We sense the overwhelming urge to strike out against those whom we despise. Sadly, these hostilities are present within our churches, among the followers of Christ. As you know, people have left the church, and separated themselves from communion with the Body of Christ, because of strong disagreements over a variety of issues. One can only imagine how this wounds the Heart of Christ. How frequently, both before and after His Resurrection, Jesus prayed for unity among His disciples. Our mission must begin here, among ourselves. From our baptism, we have been asked to walk together with Christ. Our mission is to walk together, united in mind and heart, and to walk with Him, 'He who is head of the body, the Church, is Christ.'

How true those words reflect upon the mission we have today, it is the unification of all Christians into one Universal Catholic Church as asked of us by Jesus Christ himself, to the entire world. How can we not accept this immense challenge, even knowing that we will encounter not only the powers of evil, but also the obstructions of man? But we know that with God's help He will light our way to glory in his Name.

MAY OUR LORD JESUS BLESS YOU IN THE NAME OF THE FATHER, THE SON, AND HOLY SPIRIT, MY BROTHERS AND SISTERS."

The crowds go wild with applause, cheers, dancing, and singing in St' Peter's Square, where over a million people have gathered, and the televising all over the world of this miraculous event. It is reported all over the world, by the media, concerning the event of what appeared to occur in the heavens, as reflected on the surfaces of the sun and moon. Whether in daylight or at night in any part of the earth, everyone witnessed the same thing. The awesomeness and grandeur of GOD'S power to communicate to the world at the same time was unbelievable and spectacular.

Pope John XXIV walks back into the papal apartments and views the assembled prelates in the room, looking with puzzlement as to what has just happened, and to what has been said in the media, and people in the square below. As he starts to walk into the room, he tells the assembled. "We are entering a new age of which there is no precedence, and only the Hand of God to guide us. I ask if you wish to be part of this universal church and that you are to be my instruments to its achievement, as I am a willing servant of Jesus Our Lord and God's plan. While all the Cardinals are here, we shall begin the day I am given the "Keys of St. Peter's". We have much work to do in planning and preparing for a NEW ECUMENICAL UNIVERSAL CATHOLIC CHURCH CONCLAVE meeting.

And now that it is late, I ask for your indulgence in leaving you, so that I might pray and rest?"

In the silence of the papal apartment, the new Pope kneels and prays at his private altar. He hears a gentle voice. "You have done well John, I know there will be many dark and difficult days ahead as you try to accomplish the impossible. Many will fight you every inch of the way, but I will always be at your side. And in the depths of your mind and soul, you will know my thoughts and have the wisdom to proclaim it, so that you will succeed where no one else can. Also John, I want you to get yourself a Golden Retriever for yourself, it will make you a good companion, and make sure you watch for his actions. He will help to protect you, let's say a visible guardian angel. But John, you must remember the richness of your humor and ability to enjoy life, and that must never change. Come let us take a walk so that you may nourish your soul and body to keep your strength."

CHAPTER 3

POPE JOHN XXIV'S INSTALLATION

The next day, the installation of the new Pope is being prepared, and Pope John XXIV is seen in the library working on his homily.

At the Mass, the newly installed Pope moves to the microphone. "Welcome to all who are eager to await the beginning of Christ's new age. We are to embark on a difficult journey to bring about the unity of all who are or would like to become united in an inclusive Universal Catholic Church. The Church that Jesus Christ himself founded here on earth. This will not be easy to achieve, as we all must now divest ourselves of long held beliefs and traditions that were secular and exclusive to your own church beliefs. We will not be any longer exclusive as to whom may belong or are entitled to the sacraments of the church, no longer will discrimination of any kind be allowed to those who will seek to have full membership and blessings of Jesus the Lord's Universal Catholic Church here on earth and HIS HEAVENLY KINGDOM.

One year from today, we invite representatives of all Christian, Protestant, Jewish and of other faith denominations to meet here in St. Peter's Basilica to embark on the mission of unifying all our churches into a singular faith of common tenets and beliefs as ascribed by our Lord Jesus. In order to do so, we must return to our own church ruling bodies and asks for their blessing and willingness to journey on this path. For this to succeed there has to be a determination that barriers must be removed, whether it is philosophical, historical traditions, precedents, or religious beliefs that are counter to universal inclusion. Make no mistake; this is not an exercise in futility, but one of determination that will be achieved for all who are willing to make this journey."

There is no bargaining in what the Lord is asking of us; HE IS THE WAY TO FAITH AND SALVATION. He is commanding us to achieve this NOW. And I am passing on the same challenge to every other church organization, within the Catholic Church, and every other Christian, Protestant, or other faith denominations who would want to consider a union in a Universal Catholic Church, to do the same with the members of their own church governing bodies."

At the moment of the elevation of the ciborium and chalice by the Pope, as he intones the prayer "Through him, with him, and in him, in the unity of the Holy Spirit, all glory and honor is yours, almighty Father, for ever and ever" above the Pope's head an image of the crucified Christ on the Cross is seen touching the sacred vessels, and blood dripping forth from His lanced side into the chalice. A voice proclaims from the heavens "This is my beloved Son, who gives you His body and blood at every mass, so that you may have eternal salvation, receive these gifts in remembrance of His death for you." The image of the crucifixion then disappears. The crowds go wild in exclaiming words of exaltation in every language. Some ask for forgiveness for their sins. All the media reporters and their crews are busy broadcasting to the world what just happened.

The Pope then interjects this comment. "Many, including some priests, who receive the blood and body of Christ truly never, have believed in Transubstantiation. But here and now, the true "Miracle of the Eucharist" has been shown to us by God himself."

As the Pope continues celebrating the mass, in honor of the Pope's American heritage, the assembled participants in the square, sing the hymn "Amazing Grace" and continued throughout the distribution of communion. It would appear that for the first time for many Catholics, they now truly understood the meaning of Transubstantiation of the Body and Blood of Christ occurring during each mass. They are now consuming Christ with the greatest of reverence.

As the choir is singing the final hymn, more and more in the audience are singing at the top of their lungs in glorious acclamation of the miracle that they have just witnessed. The crowds are all in a joyful and exhilarated mood as they start to disperse from the plaza.

CHAPTER 4

WOMEN AND THE CHURCH

"Americans lead in the battle for equality of the sexes in the Catholic Church. The Vatican, realizing the growing needs to legitimize women's role in the church and in the modern era, attempted to walk a fine line balancing tradition with progress. The results of these efforts left both traditionalists and modernists unsatisfied. Against the backdrop of the women's movement and the great progress that had been made in mainline Protestant churches, progressive nuns and laity demanded a larger, more visible role for women in the Catholic Church. They advocated for women to be ordained as priests and to have a greater say in church policy. These are seen as major goals in fostering equality. Nuns fighting the two-thousand-year-old, male-dominated church joined together to form groups to enhance their strength and shed their image as "docile." Organizations such as the National Assembly of Religious Women, The National Coalition of American Nuns, The Leadership Conference of Women Religious Speakers, and The Black Sisters Conference saw their membership increase, and all worked for feminist causes in and out of the church.

Another sign of the rebellion of women in the church was the sheer drop in the number of women who chose to enter convents. Seeing no hope for equality and justice in Catholicism, many young Catholic women steered away from it as a vocation. The nuns who remained in the church are highly educated, with 65 percent having master's degrees and 25 percent possessing doctorates. Conservative Catholic women, such as Phyllis Schlafly, opposed all facets of women's equality in the church and are staunch opponents of the ERA. She and many conservative Catholics have joined with fundamentalists to lobby against women's rights and abortion. Though well-funded and strident, activists such as Schlafly have grown insignificant among Catholic women as the quest for equality entered the mainstream. In 1985 Gallup polls found that 47 percent of Catholics were in favor of women priests. In 1988 U.S. Catholic bishops, realizing the need for some new official statement on women's role in the church, published the "Partners in the Mystery of Redemption." The document differed from previous bishops' documents in that some nuns were allowed to participate in discussing and drafting it, but in the end the document broke very little new ground on the issues that interested female Catholics. The church condemned sexism as a sin; yet it still did not favor women priests, contraception, or abortion. In 1989 out of desperation at the realization of the shortage of priests, the bishops issued the "Order for Sunday Celebrations in the Absence of a Priest." This decree allowed a bishop to assign a deacon or nun to lead a prayer service based on the Scriptures. Some nuns felt that this act was a first step toward real changes in the Catholic Church."

I now issue a decree from this date September 14, 2014, that the Catholic Church now will accept women as equals in the ministries performed within the episcopacies of the church government. No longer will male dominated church governance run the church. There is to be equality in membership and positions of authority throughout the church's collegial governance.

The church here on earth is to mirror Gods heavenly kingdom in who is to attain entrance. Inclusion is not based on sexual identity, race, color, creed, ethnicity, or nationality. Every human being is to have equality of membership. As Jesus said, "the first shall be last, and the last shall be first".

If we as a new church want to have a new universal Catholic church, we must start by looking internally to our own doctrines that historically were obstacles to resolving reunification efforts, with other religious traditions, in embracing the common love of our Lord Jesus Christ who came to set us free. We can no longer exclude from our membership those that do not conform to our ideas of who is a Christian. If we believe that Jesus is the Messiah that had been promised to all Christians regardless of denominations, must unite together as one people, one faith and one Universal Catholic Church."

SEXUALITY A HISTORICAL PERSPECTIVE

"The Catholic Church's condemnation of homosexuality remained historically consistent prior to the 1980s, but with the emergence of AIDS the church found that criticism of its policies intensified. One of the church's most current militant crusaders against homosexuality was New York's John Cardinal O'Connor. O'Connor, appointed in 1984, believed wholeheartedly in the strict Vatican teaching that homosexuality was a sin against God and nature. O'Connor vehemently refused an organization of gay Catholics called Dignity, to hold masses in New York churches. He also attacked the New York City Council for sponsoring a gay-rights bill that would have made it illegal to discriminate against homosexuals. In October of 1986, Joseph Cardinal Ratzinger of the Vatican issued an order forbidding Father John J. McNeill, author of the *book The Church and the Homosexual*, from preaching to the gay community and from speaking publicly about his ideas and works. McNeill's silencing followed that of Father Charles Curran the year before for his statements on sexuality, contraception, and homosexuality. The Vatican's crackdown continued on October 30, 1987, with what gay activists referred to as the "Halloween letter". It is a directive that ordered all Catholic bishops to withdraw support from any organization that opposed the official church teaching on homosexuality. Greatly impacted by this letter were many Dignity groups located across the country that used church facilities to hold their masses. Homosexual Catholics vowed to continue their services with or without official approval, as they believed it is possible to be gay and still be a good Catholic. Surveys showed that American Catholics for the most part, did not view homosexuality in the abstract as a threatening concept. Church officials held their ground, viewing homosexual acts as immoral, and were unwilling to compromise with the current sentiment. Only the epidemic of AIDS, which had caused about eighteen thousand fatalities in the United States by 1988, prompted U.S. bishops to action.

The Catholic Church, after substantial debate, allowed in 1987, for the educational discussion of the use of condoms to help control the AIDS virus. Condoms, considered a form of contraception, were previously forbidden to be discussed. Several conservative cardinals, among them Law of Boston, O'Connor of New York, and John Karol of Philadelphia, voted against the measure, believing that it condoned sex and homosexuality, but more-liberal cardinals, such as Joseph Bernardin of Chicago, pushed the issue. The question of homosexuality was also an internal one for the Catholic Church in the 1980s. Homosexual priests and nuns, exposing to the world the church's internal conflict, wrote several works. A book that caused the biggest stir in the church was the 1984 publication of the biography of the late Francis Cardinal Spellman of New York by John Cooney. The work entitled *The American Pope* exposed evidence of the cardinal's homosexuality. Another work *Lesbian Nuns: Breaking Silence* (1985) documented the stories of present and former nuns. The Catholic Church's official response to the majority of these accusations was denial."

CHAPTER 5

SUNDAY NOON AFTER THE PRAYER OF THE ANGELUS, POPE JOHN XXIV

CALLS FOR A NEW ECUMENICAL CONCLAVE FOR THE UNIVERSAL CATHOLIC CHURCH

"The College of Cardinals is to remain in Rome to start planning, developing and implementing the framework for the conversion of this new Universal Catholic Church to one of inclusion. This will be the beginning of dialogues that will culminate in the start of an Ecumenical Conclave in one year. All interested Christian, Protestant, Jewish and other denominations are welcomed to send 10 representative members, having authority to vote and recommend, to the Conclave for their consideration of doctrines and governing policies by which the Universal Catholic Church will be governed.

Yes, we as a community of believers must change in order for each and every one of its' congregants can experience fully all aspects of Christian fellowship with the Holy Trinity, in serving God Our Father, his son our Lord Jesus Christ, and the Holy Spirit. Each and every member of God's family is to have equality of love and blessings without prejudice of origin, race, color, creed, sex, and sexual orientation, single or married. The last shall be first, and the first shall be last.

It is God's will that we are to live in peace and harmony with all the people of world, and we as members of His Divine Body are to be an extension of that existence in every facet of our lives to our families, workplace, community, governments, and extending it to the limits of our universe.

This magnificent basilica is not what makes a church, but the community of believers is the church. For too long, the goal of our churches was to build monumental and glorious edifices to the glory of God, when we should have been building faith communities to spend their resources, time and energy in evangelizing the world. It will no longer be required that our priests be celibate, and they will be allowed to marry. Christ's teachings were based on the unity, strength, and love within the family. The virtues of The Holy Family have always been our model, for which we challenged our faithful to achieve. A married priesthood, experiencing the same trials and tribulations of married life, will be more knowledgeable of life, and able to share that wisdom with their flock.

Existing policies, self-centered environments, putting priests on pedestals, self glorification and seeking materialism, have led to inhumane standards that have created self-fulfilling failures within some of our priests that have led to egotism, trials, tribulations, and scandals that have rocked the church. These are prime examples of the failures of the legacy of having believed in the wrongful choices for what leads to a good, faithful, dedicated, and honored episcopacy.

Scandals have caused belligerent resentments directed at catholic churches due to behaviors as pedophilia, other sex scandals, embezzlement of church funds, etc. Fortunately, some National Bishops Conferences have accepted and addressed their responsibilities to all the innocent victims of these travesties and the need for their protection. The Universal church needs to continue to be accountable for the actions of people that represent them according to civil and legal laws of their national governments.

The purpose of a church community is not to create a means of survival, of just fulfilling our duty, but an environment for all its faithful to be nourished, emblazoned with zeal, love for our God, passion for our faith, blessings, and dedication of sharing that faith through evangelization to others and particularly to nonbelievers. Our mission here is not done. We must share our Christianity so that our love of neighbor, peace and tranquility needs to extend to all the people of this world. Our faith is not for our selffulfillment and enjoyment, we are to be servants in God's name to everyone else.

May the Peace of the Lord be with you all. In the name of the Father, The Son, and Holy Spirit, Amen."

While Pope John XXIV was speaking, everyone was quiet, but their body language easily displayed either their disbelief or awe as to what was about to happen in the church. Once he concluded his homily, everyone in the plaza goes wild with applause and excitement; the TV commentators are going ballistics with trying to capture the essence of the most outstanding statements to have ever been declared by a Pope. Members of the church Episcopacy can be seen dumbfounded by the changes being proposed by the Pope, and some are openly critical as they talk among themselves.

The Pope signals for the Choir to begin their next hymn. Slowly everyone seems to refocus on the Mass. At the conclusion of the Mass, the Pope enters the pope mobile to be among the throngs of visitors in St. Peter's Square.

As the new Pope approaches the doors of the Basilica, loud angry voices and shouts can be heard behind the closed doors. As the announcement that the Pope is entering the Basilica, everyone seems to be scrambling to disappear, and a quiet hush soon befalls the assembled.

Moving quickly towards the Pope is a group of Cardinals headed by the Dean, who upon encountering the Pope, addresses him in a terse pitch voice of displeasure.

"Your Holiness, how could you have made these ridiculous pronouncements without first consulting us, and having us vote on these matters? You are throwing the church into chaos!"
Pope John in a calm voice tells the group gathered that the College of Cardinals is to meet in the Sistine Chapel for a meeting in three hours from now, so that everyone and the staff have an opportunity to prepare as well to have a private dinner. "It will be best for all of us to gather together in order to discuss the proclamations that I

have made when all Cardinals will be present. I will meet you all there at that time, your, Excellencies."

The Pope then heads to his private chambers. With everyone standing around flustered that the Pope did not respond to their questions. Finally, they dispersed in various groups of like-minded opinions to plot their next move.

CHAPTER 6

THE SISTINE CHAPEL

Later as the Cardinals are all convening in the Sistine Chapel, with various groups in conversation, Pope John XXIV enters the Chapel, and a hush permeates the room.

Pope John XXIV, sits at his seat, there suddenly appears in the center of the Chapel, a person in a white robe, with a golden glow emanating from his body.

"My dear brothers, would you have me consult with you, before I make a proclamation? When I introduced your new Pope, I mentioned that he had MY favor. Let it be known, that when John speaks a proclamation, he is speaking for ME, your Lord God and Savior. By the conclusion of this meeting, whoever of you does not want to continue being faithful to Me in carrying out the mission of My church, needs to relinquish his position immediately, and never return to this room. John has accepted my calling; now you must also respond as to whether you will be continuing to be My disciples. This will be My last visit with you until you see me at your judgment, and until the end of the ages. But make no mistake, I am in John, and he is in Me. His discernment is My discernment." Suddenly, the Lord disappears from among their midst.

Pope John XXIV stands, and as everyone is in awe, he addresses them. "Take the remainder of your time this evening to discern what your decision is to be. Before you leave this Chapel tonight, you are to give your Lord Jesus, Our God, your answer as to whether you will continue to be 100 % His disciple. If for health reasons or other, leave your Cardinal's skull-cap on your kneeler if you are unable to make that commitment. Tomorrow, all Cardinals who have decided in the affirmative are to reconvene here at 9:00 am to continue on Our Lord's request for a Universal Catholic Church." The Pope then leaves the Chapel.

As the Cardinals leave the Sistine Chapel, all of them are in a tizzy as to what is happening, but a number of them whisper to each other to meet secretly in Cardinal Rossini's chambers. Once they have gathered in the cardinal's private chamber, Cardinal Rossini quietly states that what is discussed must be kept in complete confidence among themselves, as how to prevent this from happening to the church. They must eliminate the new Pope. So a secret plot begins among five Cardinals, who conspire to obstruct every facet of the new Pope's efforts in unifying the church. "Who can we get that will do this with upmost secrecy?" asked Cardinal Thrombus. Cardinal Rossini then expresses that he has someone in mind that is very knowledgeable of people within the Sicilian mob. "They will be very interested, obviously, for the right price of course." 'How much will this cost?' "Ah, but they will want to protect their operations! If the Church becomes any stronger and influences more participation by people, the mafia will lose revenues. The mafia will demand access to everything that is being planned, so they can do whatever to influence the right outcomes."

"We will meet again when I have more news. You must understand Cardinals that the Illuminati will also take great interest in trying to find ways to stop the Pope. Between their efforts and ours, surely one of us will succeed stopping these events."

CHAPTER 7

A NEW DAY

The bells of the Sistine Chapel began ringing, calling the Cardinals for their 9:00 am meeting. As the remaining seats are filling, except for those where the kneelers have a red skull-cap displayed for the retiring Cardinals, the Pope returns to the Chapel.

"Thank you my brothers for having the courage to embark on a new course requested by Our Lord Jesus himself to renew our church and to open its doors and windows to anyone who truly believes."

"Our task is to begin looking at what prevents the acceptance of all Christian and Protestant denominations, Jews, and the various sects within our own church into one Universal Catholic Church, that has common liturgical laws, doctrines, language, prayers, mass, sacramentals, liturgical ceremonies; so that Christian believers will be able to go to any Christian church in the entire world, and be at home in the Lord's House."

"There have been many heresies in history that have occurred by those who thought they were protecting the purity of Christ's church. One example is a Boston priest in the 1950s, which was holding vast gatherings proclaiming that only those baptized as catholic would be saved, everyone else was going to hell. He was finally excommunicated after refusing to stop. The church never professed that belief."

"We can no longer sit and expect God's work to be done miraculously, we are his disciples and it is us that need to move the mountains of obstacles that keep us from uniting all of Christ's believers. In so doing, we are bringing forth the final age of Christ's Reign. It is in our power to instill within the church membership the message that our Heavenly Father welcomes everyone. Each of you will be assigned to a new commission and administrative post to oversee the revisions necessary to make this happen, and you are relieved of prior responsibilities. As I name new Cardinals and Bishops, they also will take on new tasks in creating a new Universal Catholic Church worldwide. That task will begin today. You will only bring your completed revised doctrines and regulations to the College of Cardinals for review and approval. The final consideration and adoption of these will be by The ECUMENICAL CONCLAVE to be held next year. It will be encumbered upon you to seek Divine inspiration and wisdom in your work, to bring forth God's plan, and not those that would seek to persuade you in theirs or your own ideologies."

"The College will meet every two weeks, to consider a defined agenda of business and debate whatever completed documents submitted by you from your commissions or administrative offices. Each commission is to be formed with the same governance of membership that has been required of the current College of Cardinals. Either I or the College will appoint your new members, as our membership increases from other Christian or Protestant members, as they become part of the Universal Catholic Church."

"I will not wait for our Christian or Protestant brethren to approach us to begin a dialogue for possible unification; I will immediately seek them out, as you must also in your deliberations through your assigned commissions or administrative offices. These efforts will help you to understand the obstacles preventing other Christian faiths from joining a Universal Church. As the Lord sought out his disciples, so we must do the same."

"Peace be with you, my brothers in Christ." The Holy Father signs the Cross as he blesses them and leaves the Sistine Chapel.

CHAPTER 8

"POPE JOHN XXIV SEEKS OUT CHRISTIAN, PROTESTANT, JEWISH AND OTHER DENOMINATIONS"

Londoners read the headlines. The new Pope John XXIV is in London to meet with the Bishop of Canterbury, the Head of the Church of England, in what appears as his first attempt at reconciliation with various Christian and Protestant denominations throughout the world. It has been reported, that this week alone that the new Pontiff has scheduled meetings with every major church group willing to meet with him on their own turf. This appears to be an unprecedented approach at flaming the embers for unification.

It has also been reported by the Vatican newspaper and radio that the Pontiff has called upon all the five Catholic sects, i.e. the Greek, and Slavic Catholic Orthodox Churches, to meet in Rome for major talks on unification efforts in formulating a singular set of doctrines and liturgies that will be universal to the entire church membership, although vernacular to their own countries, but also with an English text translation subscript.

Pope John XXIV, is leaving no rock unturned, and undaunted in his efforts to open the Catholic Church to all Christian believers. A few grumblings have been heard all over the world with the inclusions of the word Catholic in the Church name, and his efforts at unification that would disrupt the status quo. The Pope appears to be welcomed by major groups of Churches in the possibility of a Universal Catholic Church.

It is understood that within the context of these talks that the Pope is having with these religious leaders, he is not only inviting them to Rome for unification talks, but also to aggressively approach their own church governing bodies to address the issues that would prevent unification of a single church. This would seem an impossible task considering the various splinter groups that have developed over the centuries and particularly these last few years, within those churches with issues dealing with sexual orientation membership, gay clergy, pro-life, etc. With so many divisive issues it will certainly take a miracle to get any of these polarized factions to enter into a mutually inclusive united church.

It would seem impossible for one man to attempt such an enormous undertaking, but he certainly appears energized with heavenly powers for the tasks. He reminds us of the heroic attempts by his predecessor Pope John XXIII, who masterly called for the Conclave to modernize the Catholic Church back in the 1960's. But in comparison, this is not like building a single house, but that of building the tallest skyscraper in the world.

CHAPTER 9

IN THE DEN OF CO-CONSPIRITORS

"Cardinal Rossini, I understand from my lieutenants, that you wanted to meet personally. But you wouldn't discuss any details with them. But forgive the hood; it was necessary to keep this location secret."

"Yes, Giovanni Jesuppi, I have come here in secret to discuss great matters that may affect your financial wellbeing, if the plans by the new Pope ever come to pass. Your empire cannot exist if the Church becomes more popular and powerful. If the faithful become more zealous in their faith, you will lose your clients."

"But Cardinal Rossini, you must jest, how can such a thing ever happen in this materialistic world? People love greed, sex, power; I can't believe that would ever change." "But it could Giovanni, if this Pope is allowed to succeed. That is why I have come to beg you to enjoin your resources, here and abroad, to find ways to kill the new Pope, and prevent his plans from taking hold. I know you have your resources and contacts.
Surely you can understand the implications, if this were allowed to occur."

"Well, Cardinal Rossini, I will consider your arguments and see what can be done in our mutual interest, with my worldwide resources. But you must understand that we also act in secrecy, and things will happen without your knowledge or ability to stop once things happen. So do not attempt to contact us again, or there will be repercussions."

"By all means Giovanni, thank you." "Thank you! My men, Cardinal Rossini will escort you again in secret to a private location."

THE ILLUMINATI

A vastly different type of group is meeting secretly within the chambers of the Vatican. Their heads cloaked in monks habit to help shield their identities, sit in a circular series of numbered chairs. Their robust chatter is protected from roving ears by the soundproof room. The discussions focused on the paradox of their need for extreme secrecy, protecting the status quo, and now with the new revelations by Jesus Himself asking for an about face of how and by whom the church will govern itself at the exclusion of others.

Number 22 stands and exclaims. "These are truly unprecedented times as revealed by the recent miracles. This has been a declaration of war! Our way of life and control will be demolished if we do not take effective actions to stop the new pope from putting in all these changes as he is proposing."

"I know as you do that there are a number of cardinals who are very unhappy with the changes that are going to take place, and will do whatever they can to prohibit them from taking place. I, for one, understand their displeasure. I will be among them to keep tabs on their efforts. But we have worldwide resources and contacts to derail any of the Pope's plans. We need to be vigilant and assist in making sure any of their plans will be individually successful; however, surrepticiliously in order to keep our actions and identity secret. If your actions are insufficient please get more of our members involved and use our resources. If you agree, raise your hands!"

"By your unanimous agreement, this is now our direction. For the sake of the

continued existence of the Illuminati, we must not fail, and as always be vigilant. We will send out an immediate alert worldwide to our extended network for their vigilance in support of this action." In the order of their assigned seat, they rise in succession of five minutes apart, in order to not raise suspicion of their identities or whereabouts to each other or outsiders. As they leave the inner chamber, they pass into an antechamber leaving their cloak and proceeding out of one of thirteen locked doors to various parts of the Vatican secret corridors, catacombs, or confessional passages. In order to guarantee their secrecy, the antechamber is setup to light a light on each side of a door to indicate its use by an individual. The locks are also set up to allow only one person at a time to enter the chamber from outside entrances. Because of the locations of the thirteen doors, no one can see any of the other entrances from any one door.

CHAPTER 10

GLOBAL NEWSCAST: POPE JOHN XXIV'S VEHICLE IS BLOWN UP

An attempted assassination, by an unknown person or groups, of Pope John XXIV occurred today in Rome on his way to the papal summer residence. Fortunately, although his armored vehicle sustained major damage, the Pope was removed from the vehicle by his security guards following his vehicle, and appeared unscathed from the attempt. He was rushed to the hospital for observation, but was soon released and went on to his summer residence.

Rumors have circulated that there have been other attempts on his life, but he seems undaunted and insists on continuing with his enormously busy schedule. It would appear that there seems to be organized efforts too interrupt his efforts at uniting the world Christian churches.

The pontiff's schedule has been kept more secret since these attempts, and therefore meetings with other church leaders worldwide appear to be more of clandestine operations. One would expect such efforts considering whom the Pope is meeting, not only for his safety, but also the leaders he is attempting to persuade.

While Pope John XXIV is pacing in his study, a gentle hand rests on his shoulder, with a slight fright; he turns to see the Lord. "John, remember my Angels and I are with you at all times. There are many who will attempt to try to kill you, even within the episcopacy, but they will not succeed." 'Yes, my Lord, I take comfort in that, but as you know I'm only mortal and it does make my heart go pitter patter every so often.' "Sleep well my son!"

CHAPTER 11

THE CHURCH IS EUPHORIC

Pope John XXIV names 75 new Cardinals to be installed at a ceremony in Rome. The lists includes numerous clergy both men and women, and some married individuals from around the world, including prominent theologians from Protestant denominations. It has been reported that among those announced are individuals that have been recommended by their respective churches as delegates to the Holy See. It would appear that the new Pope is indeed fulfilling his promises of including these nominees as part of the College of Cardinals in forming a new Universal Catholic Church.

The ongoing discussions with world Christian churches appear to be developing at unprecedented speeds, unheard of in the slow and methodical discernments of past church history. This Pope has indeed galvanized his church leadership and its members to truly embrace God's request for a unified church. It is absolutely amazing that these events are occurring all over the Christian world. Even among the faithful of various congregations there is a renewed spirit of faith that appears contagious, and is spreading like raging wild fires.

There have been outrageous demonstrations by various organized groups attempting to slow or stop the unification efforts in every Christian church. But so far, the vast majority of Christians seem emboldened in fulfilling the request of the Lord God Himself when appearing in Rome to announce the new Pope, of His desire for a Universal Catholic Church. Everything is happening at a feverish pitch.

ST PETER'S BASILICA, ROME

Among massive security efforts in the installation of the 75 new Cardinals named by Pope John XXIV, the celebration is occurring in the Basilica instead of the square, as has been the custom. This is a most remarkable time in the church in breaking with centuries of tradition by naming female and married individuals to the College of Cardinals, including the Patriarch of Constantinople, the Archbishop of Canterbury, and the Elder from the Mormon Faith. It is our understanding that the non-Catholic prelates will first be asked to confirm their allegiance to the Pope, and then conferred Holy Orders as priests within the Catholic Church. The final ceremony will be the presentation of the Red Hat, designating their installation as Cardinals within the Catholic Church.

It is also unprecedented, at such an event, that there appears to be an organized protest crowd of hundreds in St. Peter's square attempting to disrupt the proceedings. They have placards denouncing the Pope as Satan or with other sacrilegious names. The papal guards as well as the police from Rome are attempting to keep the protesters quarantine to one area, in order to maintain control and away from the thousands of faithful in the crowds.

The Vatican paper, "l'OSSERVATORE ROMANO", has also mentioned that the entire College of Cardinals would be starting deliberations tomorrow on a vast array of topics, as well as decisions to be made regarding the unifications of various worldwide Christian and Protestant churches, that have been in dialogue with the Holy See. These are unprecedented times bringing forth such diverse groups and resulting in the polarization of diverse opinions. It appears in the final analysis, that these developments are gaining acceptance for the unification of all groups who believe in the same God. This new Pope certainly has been working tirelessly for the unification process, although many critics within the Catholic Church feel he is betraying historical traditions and precedents.

CHAPTER 12

RUMORS ABOUND OF VARIOUS ATTEMPS ON POPE JOHN XXIV'S LIFE

Various individuals have been questioned by legal authorities on suspicions of plots on the life of the Pope. It has been rumored that some of his food and liquids have been found tainted with poisons, and that "various accidents" have threatened His life. Apparently his vehicle has been sabotaged, and objects have mysteriously fallen just missing the Pontiff. Thankfully his papal security forces have been very successful in protecting him.

Pope John asks some of the Cardinals to dinner one evening. As the custom for such a meal, a number of wine bottles were brought by a number of guests. During the meal, Peter, the Pope's new dog laid by his feet. Next to the Pope was Cardinal Pompeii, who asked if he could pour the Pontiff wine. "Why yes, that would be great, thank you Cardinal." All of a sudden Peter gets up and puts his head and presses on the Pope's arm, just as he was about to take his first sip of wine. "Oh Peter, would you like some wine too?' "You'll have to excuse me your Excellencies while I go to the kitchen and get a saucer for Peter." "But no, no, your Holiness, that is very expensive wine, retorted Cardinal Pompeii, it would be such a waste." "Oh I'm sure Cardinal Pompeii, Peter will greatly appreciate that he's becoming a great Connoisseur." As the Pope, nears the sink in the kitchen, he exclaims, "Oh how gauche of me, I just spilled my wine into this plant, and oh it seems to be wilting, and I was going to give some to Peter." As soon as the cook hears this, he rushes to the Pope, and brings a new bottle of wine for him. Upon his return, with a saucer, he puts it on the floor for Peter, and pours a spoonful of wine for him. Cardinal Pompeii keeps looking at Peter as he licks the saucer, and starts to sweat profusely. After a few minutes he asks the Pontiff if he can be excused since all of a sudden he feels ill.

Cardinal Pompeii quickly scribbles a note of what happened at dinner and leaves it under Cardinal Rossini's room door as he goes by in the hallway. The next day they are both walking in the corridor, and see Peter strutting by. They both gasp, putting the hands to their mouth, and whispering, "But he should be dead." Quickly they look about to see if anyone else saw them, and then briskly walk away to their rooms.

On the eve of the College of Cardinals meeting with the newly installed Cardinals, Cardinal Rossini is secretly meeting with his co-conspirators. The other Cardinals appear to be very frustrated and are gripping with Cardinal Rossini, in that the new Pope is very much alive and that their grip on power will now be diluted with the new group of Cardinals. Cardinal Rossini is trying desperately to calm them down and telling that he too is very disappointed. Finally in trying to dispel their fears, he tells them that he has arranged for the Sicilian mob to take the necessary arrangements to have the Pope killed. Events have shown that numerous attempts have been made, yet unsuccessful, they are still trying. Some Cardinals express fear that they could then become targets also of the Sicilians.

Cardinal Rossini continues to attempt to calm their fears, but admonishes them to make sure they continue to vote in unison, in order to control any outcome of the proceedings and to follow his lead within deliberations of the College of Cardinals.

CHAPTER 13

THE SISTINE CHAPEL BELLS RINGS

All the Cardinals are beginning to assemble in the Sistine Chapel for the new session that is to start. As they mingle congratulating the new members, Pope John XXIV enters the chapel and joins in mingling with the new Cardinals. With members from all around the world speaking in various tongues, it seems to sound very much like a meeting of the United Nations Assembly. Thankfully a new translation system has been installed, to make sure everyone understands the presentations.

Finally the Dean of the College of Cardinals calls for all to take their assigned seats followed by prayers of thanksgiving, and instructs them to open and peruse the packets in front of them of the itinerary of topics to be discussed.

Pope John XXIV stands to address the assembly.

"My dear brothers and sisters in Christ Jesus, today we embark on the discernment of the Universal Catholic Church as Christ and God has asked us. This would not have been possible without your willingness to participate and take us all on a new path to unification. Many of your concerns and recommendations have been carefully reviewed and thoroughly considered and hopefully will have been expressed appropriately in the doctrines and church laws that now appear in the documents prepared for your consideration. Please pray and reflect upon them, consulting your colleagues, etc., before we start deliberating tomorrow afternoon at 2:00 p.m. There are many items, some of which will be more profound in nature for you than others, but we will take them up in the order they were presented on the itinerary. We will only consider two items at most on any given day, taking appropriate time with each even if it requires more than one day of deliberating, and voting on that particular item before going onto the next. Please be thoroughly prepared for each item, as this will be the only time we will discern that subject during our sessions. At the conclusion of our sessions, all items voted in the affirmative will be printed and sent to you, so that you may present them to your various church governing bodies for their consideration, and in consultations with the Holy See if required. For all of you representing your church organization, once all the doctrines and governing laws meet with their approval, and they wish to be become part of the Universal Catholic Church, please have them approve and sign the Unification Acceptance Doctrine for submittal to the Holy See. There is no deadline for submittal other than your own. Proper deliberation, full acceptance, and compliance are required for total union with the Holy See.

Peace be with you and may the Lord God bless you and keep you in the palm of his hands in the name of the Father, The Son and The Holy Spirit."

CHAPTER 14

THE GANG OF FIVE

The "gang of five" is secretly meeting with Cardinal Rossini. Cardinal Doyen asked the group. "How can we continue with the plans? There is security everywhere and we're bound to be discovered." Cardinal Rossini expresses, 'Yes it is very dangerous, but I am certain that it can be done. We have to have the Pope travel out of the city under some pretext so that he will be in a more vulnerable environment to an attack. I'll personally take it upon myself, to escort him on his trip.' "But will you not also be in danger?" 'There is some risk, Cardinal Lyon, but I'll take extra precautions. Quickly you must all return to your own suites from different directions in order to maintain our secrecy.'

Cardinal Rossini calls to the Papal apartment. "Your Holiness, it is such a beautiful day, why don't we take a ride into the countryside to get some fresh air. The heat here in Rome is somewhat oppressive." 'Well that sounds like a good plan, however give me about an hour to clear my itinerary and I'll be ready to join you Cardinal Rossini. I'll get my chauffer to prepare the car for us.'

Cardinal Rossini enters his suite to prepare for his trip and puts on a bulletproof vest. This is great; it will give me time to call Giovanni regarding my plans. "Giovanni this is Cardinal Rossini, I've made plans for the Pope and me to take a drive to the country in order to give your men the opportunity to do as you plan. But remember to tell your men, I'll also be in the car, and not to shoot at me." 'I hear you, Cardinal; I'll let them know.'

"Ah it is very refreshing to be out in the countryside, Cardinal Rossini, thank you for suggesting it. My schedule has been so busy; I have not had the time for a break."

Suddenly a black vehicle approaches the Pope's vehicle from behind after having pushed the Papal Swiss Guard security vehicle off the road, and nudges quickly alongside, then cuts in front as they come to a screeching halt. Two men rush out of the vehicle and approach the Pope, knocking on the vehicle doors with their automatic weapons, telling the Pope to get out. The Pope in the back seat looks out the window with amazement. "But I'm sorry, my security people tell me never to get out unless they are the ones to open the door." The assailants keep knocking and then suddenly open fire on the vehicle.

"Oh look at this Cardinal Rossini, isn't this fascinating! I have just received this new armored vehicle from the US Government, and they tell me that this is as secure as the President of the USA own' vehicle. It is made to withstand any type of weapon or surface to air missiles. I didn't believe that I would need such a vehicle, but the President himself called and asked that I accept it." The gunmen after ten minutes of firing on the vehicle go and get a "surface to air missile". After firing the missile to no avail, they finally hunch their shoulders and decide to leave. "Oh my, Cardinal Rossini, hasn't this been an adventure like those special effects movies." '"Yes, yes, but I'm perspiring and sweating so that I'm all wet and need to go to the bathroom right away." "Oh, by all means Cardinal Rossini." 'Percy, please drive us back quickly!' "This has been the most excitement I've had in quite some time, Cardinal." "Oh, Cardinal, it is odorous in here! Please, OOOopen the windows!!!"

No sooner had the Pope's vehicle turned back for the Vatican, another menacing looking military type vehicle approaches and starts bumping the Pope's car. Cardinal Rossini starts yelling to the driver to drive faster. They are now both speeding faster and faster and weaving back and forth between other vehicles. Cars are being forced off the road into ditches and into other parked cars. As the vehicles now head into a straight stretch of road, the military van speeds up next to the Pope's vehicle. The van's side door opens with a volley of automatic gunfire hitting the Pope's car and ricocheting in all directions. But none of the bullets are piercing through the armor. Next the terrorist attacks the Pope's vehicle by extending a metal pole out with a bomb with a magnet that attaches itself to the Pope's car. The terrorists suddenly veer off and quickly break to allow distance between both vehicles. The Illuminati member in the military van then presses a trigger to explode the bomb. There's a huge explosion but the Pope's car keeps on going with no penetration into the vehicle. The Pope calls out to Cardinal Rossini, "Are you OK Cardinal?" The Cardinal starts to look and feels his arms and legs, not believing what just happened. 'Yes, yes I am ok, but a bit shook up. This can't be happening. How are we still alive?' Suddenly, a military helicopter appears in front of the Pope's car and launches a missile at the military van and blows it up. The helicopter pilot then comes over the Pope's radio speaker system, advising the Pope that the threat has been eliminated and they will escort him back to the Vatican.

The Pope then quietly prays a prayer of thanksgiving, and exclaims to Cardinal Rossini that this is probably enough of a venture for one day.

CHAPTER 15

CONTROVERSAL DECISIONS BY THE COLLEGE OF CARDINALS

The Vatican newspaper the l'Osservatore Romano, has reported that The College of Cardinals has been able to review and approve numerous controversial doctrines and administrative regulations, including allowing priests to be married, eliminating the centuries old requirement of celibacy, allowing female priests, homosexual or lesbian priests, and allowing previously ordained priests, who left to marry or for other reasons, to return to the priesthood.

One major decision has included the reunification of all the major sects within the Catholic Church, that of the Maronites, Greek Catholics, Roman Catholics, Greek Orthodox, Syrian Orthodox, Armenian Orthodox, Assyrian or Nestorian, and minor sects comprised of Chaldean Catholics, Bahais, Armenian Catholics, Copts, Turkomans, Circassians, and Opus Dei to be governed and to follow the revised singular universal doctrines and regulations of the Universal Catholic Church with an English translation and the vernacular of the country of origin for all liturgical events.

The College of Cardinals has also approved the acceptance of the following major groups' international religious entities: The Anglican Church of England, Episcopal Church of the United States, Lutheran Church Of America and Lutheran National Congregations and its affiliates from Europe, and will be continuing to review on an ongoing basis all applications of other denominational churches from around the world wanting to join.

All sacraments validly celebrated within the liturgical customs of each denomination, such as marriages, baptisms, confirmations are deemed valid in the Universal Catholic Church. Holy Orders, which is the sacrament reserved for the ordination of priests, will however require security and criminal background reviews, passing a theological exam of the revised church doctrines and regulations, and pledge of obedience to the Pope, upon receiving the Rite of Holy Orders. This is so that all clergy will be able to officially preside at a Mass or any other sacramental rites celebrated in any of the churches, considered part of the Universal Catholic Church. It will also be the intent of removing non-pastoral duties from all clergy and making that the responsibility of shared centralized administrative secular organizations for multiple church clusters, including any governing bodies within the designated episcopacies of various churches conferences.

All extraordinary ministers, teachers, all employees in whatever capacity in any programs associated or conducted in churches, schools, or other buildings owned by the churches, will be required to pass a security and criminal background check.

Real estate properties will continue to be owned, and any liabilities associated with them, will belong and continue to be the responsibilities of the existing church denominations, and will not be transferred to any Catholic Diocese.

Any employee compensation or benefit plan will continue as they exist, until such time as an appropriate study can be concluded, that will be able to provide a comprehensive equitable compensation and benefit plan for all employees and clergy.

All theological institutions associated with the formation and preparation for all clergy for all church denominations, that have been accepted as part of the Universal Catholic Church will now be guided by the current doctrines and regulations accepted by the College of Cardinals.

All church denominations, that are accepted as part of the Catholic Universal Church must sign a joint formal written agreement documenting their declaration of acceptance of the Doctrines, Church Laws, and Regulations governing the Catholic Universal Church, and their acceptance of the Pope as their spiritual leader.

L'Osservatore Romano, the Vatican paper, reports that the volume of dignitaries from around the world representing various Christian and Protestant denominations that have come to St. Peter's has been monumental. Every conceivable hotel, motel, bed and breakfast facility, as well as every available convent, rectory, boarding school, and college housing facility have been recruited to provide housing and dining facilities for these representatives. Every conceivable vendor and business establishment within a hundred miles from Rome, report that business incomes have been a bonanza never seen in their lifetimes. It has also been noted that at every Catholic Church, in and outside of Rome, have been holding masses every hour around the clock in order to accommodate all the visiting faithful to Rome.

Even the normal scheduled appearances by the Pope have been indefinitely suspended for the foreseeable future. It has been reported that the Pope has a sixteen-hour daily schedule of appointments meeting with various groups, reviewing documents, and is currently booked well into next year. A new web site has been established to identify major recent developments with various worldwide Christian, Jewish, and Protestant church denominations that have signed acceptance agreements to become part of the Universal Catholic Church. Copies of all finalized documents and documents now in progress are included on the website, in order to make sure everyone is up to date on the latest events. Every major tentative religious website associated with the Universal Catholic Church has been reported to include announcements of major events of all the various Christian and Protestant denominations that have agreed to join the Universal Catholic Church.

Pope John XXIV has booked the following stadiums for a mass and appearance on:

DATE   LOCATION   CAPACITY

September 1, 2014 St. Peter's Square, Vatican, Rome, Italy 150,000

September 4, 2014 Michigan Stadium, Ann Arbor, Michigan USA 109,901

September 7, 2014 Olympic Stadium, Montreal, Canada 66,308

September 10, 2014 Estadio Azteca, Mexico City, Mexico 105,000

September 16, 2014 Bukit Jalil National Stadium, Kuala Lumpur, Malaysia 100,200

September 19, 2014 Eden Gardens, Kolkata, India 90,000

September 22, 2014 Salt Lake Stadium, Kolkota, India 120,000

September 25, 2014 Azadi Stadium, Tehran, Iran 100,000

September 28, 2014 Gelora Bung Karno, Jakarta, Indonesia 88,306

October 1, 2014 Borg El Arab Stadium, Alexandria, Egypt 86,000

October 4, 2014 Guangdong Olympic Stadium, Guanghou, China 80,012

October 7. 2014 Olimpiysky National Sports Complex, Kiev, Ukraine 83,160

October 10, 2014 Luzhniki Stadium, Moscow, Russia 75,000

October 13, 2014 Signal Iduna Park, Dortmund, Germany 81,264

October 16, 2014 Alliaz Arena, Munich, Germany 69,901

October 19, 2014 Athens Olympic Stadium, Athens, Greece 71,030

October 22, 2014 Estadio do Maracana, Rio de Janeiro, Brazil 82,238

October 25, 2014 Estadio Monumental, Lima, Peru 80,093

October 28, 2014 Abuja Stadium, Abuja, Nigeria 60,000

November 1, 2014 Stade Mohamed V, Casablanca, Morocco 80,000

November 4, 2014 Stade des Martyrs, Kinshasa, Congo 80,000

November 7, 2014 King Fahd International Stadium, Riyadh, Saudi Arabia67, 000

November 10, 2014 Mad Day Stadium, Pyongyang, North Korea 150,000

November 13, 2014 International Stadium, Yokohama, Japan 70,000

November 16, 2014 Melbourne Cricket Ground, Melbourne, Australia 100,018

November 19, 2014 Wembley Stadium, London, UK 90,000

November 22, 2014 Croke Park, Dublin, Ireland 82,300

November 25, 2014 Swedbank Arena, Stockholm, Sweden 65,000 November 28, 2014 Stade de France, Paris France 81,264

No appearances by the Pope have been planned during the month of December 2014. It is reported that scheduled visits to other countries will be planned after the Easter Holidays in 2015, to give the Pope time to meet with the College of Cardinals upon his last stadium appearance. Even though the listed stadium capacities are listed, it is anticipated that thousands more will fill the playing fields of these stadiums, and therefore it is unknown what the total attendance could be. It is also anticipated that millions more faithful will be viewing these live telecasts of the appearances by Pope John XXIV.

The security precautions for the Pope's travels have been unprecedented, including consultations with the secret service of the President of the United States. It is understood also that a new plane and armored vehicle has been ordered under tight security with the latest safety measures. It is well known that there have been numerous assassination attempts on his life, but he insist on making these planned appearances. All of the planned trips are also being coordinated with national security organizations of the countries being visited.

CHAPTER 16

POPE JOHN XXIV'S ADDRESS AT BUKIT JALIL NATIONAL STADIUM
IN KUALA LUMPUR, MALAYSIA

SEPTEMBER 16, 2014 MARRIAGE & THE FAMILY

My dear brothers and sisters, our Lord Jesus was raised by Our Blessed Mother and Saint Joseph, commonly designated as our Holy Family. They have provided us the perfect example of truly unique characteristics to inspire and guide our homes, our extended families, our communities, our work environments, our nations, and in particular our religious life in the Universal Catholic Church. God provided a means for us to have a human representation for us to witness his existence through the image of the Holy Family. Jesus lived here on Earth among us to reveal the love of Our Father, and established his Church by which we could become a family with His heavenly kingdom. This Church is the manifestation of our religious family of believers just as the Trinity reveals the glorification of The Father, the humanity of The Son and the transformative power of the Holy Spirit. God not only provided a human son, to see, hear, and witness, but also provided the Holy Spirit, that lives within our soul. So not only is Jesus his Son, but we also are the Children of God. You and I are Family. We are part of GOD'S HOLY FAMILY.

The Sacrament of Marriage goes beyond conferring marital and parental rights and obligations, by producing the same supernatural effects as the other six sacraments: it increases sanctifying grace and leads to actual graces throughout the duration of the marriage. Since GOD unites Himself to the married couple, the grace of GOD dwells within them and the manifestation of holiness is increased. With this sacrament, natural love is elevated above the earthly and placed upon the Altar of GOD. Non-believers of the existence of God cannot equate with the values exhibited by the Church within the Sacrament of Marriage, or to how others define a civil marriage in various cultures.

With over 50 % of marriages ending in divorce worldwide, including within the church, we ourselves need to revitalize all the values we place on the sacraments of the church, so that our members truly understand its significance in their lives. How can the church be involved heavily in politicizing the definition of civil marriages for non-Catholics when we are failing to strengthen its values within our own church? Over the centuries the church itself has struggled with which union of couples was acceptable. "Mixed marriages" were discouraged or not allowed to be performed within a traditional Catholic Mass. The various issues raised by orthodox believers, and the assimilation of races, cultures, creed, or class systems in some societies have cause tremendous upheavals in the lives of people. Even today that dialogue is often centered on the same sex marriage issues.

When God made Eve, he did not define the word "marriage", but simply would have been defined today as a "common-law marriage" even though the term marriage did not exist at that time. "For this reason a man shall leave his father and mother and be joined to his wife, and the two shall become one flesh. So they are no longer two, but one flesh. Therefore, what GOD has joined together, no human must separate." Matthew 19:5-6.

As Christ has indicated that gays in fact were born that way, God gives them the same rights and privileges as any other individual. So let it be that same sex marriages will be allowed in the Catholic churches, whereas these committed individuals will have the same nurturing Christian teachings and graces enjoyed by heterosexual couples married in the church.

God not only created a companion for Adam, but also the means for procreation. The church teachings have traditionally proclaimed that the primary purpose of sex in marriage must always be that of procreation. In God's creation of sex in the ecological and biological world, it is part of natural existence and not an evil action. Sex within the marriage of two human beings is historically professed as of a God given function. However the intrinsic value we place on a Christian, marriage must be celebrated through the grace of intimacy shared in a loving relationship which nature does not provide in the purely physical action. For a marriage to succeed as an everlasting union, the natural physical expression needs to continue to strengthen the bonds of the spiritual relationship of the couple, beyond the natural period of procreation. It is a physical relationship that can extend to the twilight years of the couple until physical limitations occur.

In the church's proclamation of the sanctity of a marriage between two individuals, it has nevertheless overreached by its intrusion in dealing with the actions of sexual activity, or of birth control measures practiced by a couple. The only area that the church rightly needs to reaffirm the sanctity of life is to oppose abortions, which destroys the life of an embryo in the womb or invitro, capital punishment and euthanasia. On the issue of scientific or medical research, as long as embryos in vitro are not destroyed, the church does not prohibit its development.

There is no prohibition of the type of birth control utilized except for when it would destroy an embryo. The use of contraceptives to control world populations is an acceptable measure in the ability of the world to feed the poor and those plagued by hunger, and avoid worldwide famines.

The church teaching that sex in marriage is only for procreation does not recognize that sex is a God given gift and part of the nature of man. The continued enjoyment by a couple of the gift of sexuality should not be restricted after a couple is no longer able or desirous to not have additional children. The church's teachings relative to a couple's sexual activities should not be on the basis of ancient practices of abstinence or the rhythm method of birth control. The use of modern day birth control practices, except for those that would cause abortions, is acceptable for Catholics.

The ability to enjoy sex, which is a God given gift, should not be restricted by a spouse's inabilities or the church condemnation. That is a deeply personal decision by a couple, and should not be regulated by church teachings.

In the early evolution of the family, the size of a family was conditional on the economic survival of a family, because having children enabled families to expand the productivity and cultivation of farms or other agronomic economies that existed at that time without the need of external labor sources.

Today's families do not generally produce their own food or other products necessary to maintain a family. The majority of families live in cities or industrialized environments, where economies require earning a livelihood. This allows families to purchase their food, shelter, clothing, or other necessary products. So the size of families is generally based on their ability to function within these economic realities.

In the United States, the controversial Roe v. Wade Supreme Court ruling that allowed for legal abortions has caused over 55 million deaths of babies in this country. The choices made by anti-abortion rights groups in trying to pray, civil disobedience, marches or blowing up abortion clinics or killing doctors has not stemmed the tide of continued abortions. We need to adopt a different approach for a solution to this horrific crime against babies. This is a worldwide problem that must be dealt with.

The church needs a positive loving and compassionate proactive approach to world nations to control population overgrowth, and in helping all females considering active sexual involvement to utilize whatever birth control devices or medications to prevent unintended births. Second, programs must be implemented that gives mothers information about other viable options, other than resorting to abortions, whether through an adoption process, education, or assistance in finding whatever resources they can acquire that will help them become good parents, and providers for their new families. One program would be to initiate non-threatening facilities that provide a shelter, free of spiritual guidance for non-Catholics, but help provide resources for the mother till she delivers her baby, and finally decides to keep the baby or chooses adoption. By providing positive alternative resources, we might have a better chance in stemming the tide of abortions worldwide then outright confrontations, that tend to harden the opinions of prochoice zealots.

Our God is a loving and compassion Father, we as a church need to deal with the issues surrounding abortion, whether with the mothers, the medical community, or our communities in a similar way, so that we can reverse the tide of pro-choice proponents. There is a better way to deal with unwanted pregnancies then to resorting to the use of abortions. It is very evident that violent confrontation is not working to solve this problem. Nor will it be resolved through the legal court process.

The issue of divorce of married couples, who have been married in the church, should not be any different than for a priest who can no longer be allowed to perform sacraments in the church. In the past a catholic, whose marriage ended in a civil divorce was required to abstain from receiving the Eucharist. The only option for that person to continue receiving the Eucharist was to obtain an annulment. The process of annulments should be changed to allow for dissolution of a church marriage with the same guidelines of a civil divorce. With over 50 % of all marriages being dissolved in civil courts, it gives credence that Catholics will also have dissolutions. The church needs to be a place of comfort, caring and mediation for all such families affected by divorce, particularly if children are involved. We must do a better job in helping families in receiving supported services that will help minimize the debilitating effects affecting families who face divorce. The Church has to be an extension of that family, providing a loving, caring, and nurturing resource for them. Divorced individuals should never be ostracized by others. Church ministry should include helping each other when difficulties arise among its members. The dissolution of a family is one of the greatest difficulties that anyone can experience. It can lead to desperation, depression, financial catastrophe, illnesses, children abandonment, aggression, physical harm or death. These are not minor circumstances. They are very acute situations that can have lasting impact. The church needs to be proactive in helping families deal with these issues, and not be a bystander.

CHAPTER 17

POPE JOHN XXIV'S ADDRESS AT GELORA BUNG KARNO, IN JAKARTA, INDONESIA ON SEPTEMBER 28, 2014

CONTROVERSIES OF GRACE VS FREE WILL

Do you believe in God? If you do, we are not alone. God is everywhere. Our souls are the repository of the Holy Spirit. The Saints and Angels are among us, helping us in our time of need. Our dearly departed whose lives merited eternal life are with God. They are there to watch and intercede for us, so we are never alone.

The souls in purgatory are being purified. They are not in hell, for that is for those who are eternally dammed. So where is purgatory? Many have believed that living in some cases has been pure hell, or too difficult with circumstances beyond their control. Have the lives of our Saints been without trials, tribulations, and some cases martyrdom?

Purgatory exists as a spirit world side by side among the living. We do not see them, but they are spending time among us to gain purification for their stained souls, doing those things by which they would have merited eternal life if they had done so while living, earning their wings so to speak. Unlike prisoners in society who earned time for good behavior, are paroled, but who nevertheless having not changed their characters or behavior are often doomed to repeat the process. Purgatory is not a cleansing fire to gain parole, but one which allows the souls to attempt to influence the living to respond with grace and dignity in the way of the Lord. It is just and proper that we continue to pray for these souls, so that they finally experience eternal union with the Creator.

The fallen angel, the demon, exists in our world, to capture or entice souls with greed, lust, murder, and to sin against all the commandments of God or church teachings guiding them against what is good and divine. So there is within the world all manner of evil worshipers and servants of the devil, including the demon. They are out there enticing future followers.

All Christian believers must be diligent in every aspect of their lives to lead wholesome lives, and to seek the strength of the sacraments and grace from the Trinity to remain strong on their life's journey to eternal salvation. There is no shortcut to heaven. It is truly a life of struggles, heartaches, and immeasurable difficulties to achieve success toward our heavenly reward. However, if we follow the examples of the saints, and accept the burdens of life, we can also gain the graces to endure those struggles by the generosity of spirit. Consider the "Beatitudes" in your life struggles; their truths enable us to be beneficiaries of their wisdom in understanding the meaning of sacrifices. For when you see the fruits of your labors, you will rejoice in the Spirit of God and that will nourished your souls to keep on the journey.

Many cry out with vengeance at God for causing world catastrophes and heinous tragic events in people's lives. God is not the cause of these tragedies, but the evil forces at work all over the world, and those that would sabotage our earthly, monetary, and physical entities of world structures, governments, and human beings for their own selfishness or grandiosity. If one looks at some of the horrific calamities that have occurred in the world, you need only look at the horrors of wars and the reasons countries go to war. When a life is taken by another, the repercussions felt by the peoples whose lives are touched by that person, causes immeasurable harm and difficulties for possibly a lifetime of events. It is like a stone thrown in a pond and the waves it creates; human lives are changed forever. In natural cataclysmic disasters such as earthquakes, floods, hurricanes, devastating fires covering hundreds of miles it is often exacerbated by human decisions of peoples or governments that have long term influences like climate change that impact thousands or millions of lives around the world. It is the iconic struggle of evil vs. good, devil vs. God.

Greed results in companies or persons choosing to compromise economic principles or structures with inferior materials in order to have a greater profit, at the risk of people's lives if that structure fails. Ethnic genocide, territorial disputes, earthly treasures all have contributed to conflicts of war and devastation.

This is why our Lord Jesus has come back to us, to reverse the direction we as humans must change in order to save our world from its own destruction. We as Christian must unite as one, to give people and their leaders the examples by which we can live in peaceful co-existence. To succeed will be to eliminate wars, atrocities, famines and evil from this world. It is not an easy task, but it is what our Lord Jesus is asking us to do. Unlike the crusades of the early church, this is not about military might, but one of persuading others of what the Christian spirit and beliefs are all about.

CHAPTER 18

POPE JOHN XXIV'S ADDRESS AT UNITED NATIONS GENERAL ASSEMBLY, NEW YORK CITY, NEW YORK

ON SEPTEMBER 5, 2014 WAR & PEACE

Is there justification for war? In the history of mankind, there is no major decade in which a war did not occur somewhere around the world. All human life must be valued from conception to death. All wars are inhuman. Those who would wage war have no regard for human life and see it as a necessary evil of inflicting conflict on others for avengement of an attack, or for winning territories. They are guilty of the most heinous of acts against God and humanity. Countries around the world that have or intend to possess the means of creating a nuclear, biological, or other weapon of mass destruction do so with the intent of creating a holocaust through the annihilation of its enemies. No country in the world is safe from sabotage by terrorist, who would want to provoke war for their own purposes, for power, or greed. Those who have these weapons in the name of self-preservation or as a deterrent are only deceiving themselves. Because they exist, the threat of even accidental nuclear, chemical, energized weapons sources can result in a holocaust as a result of human error, whether financial, unintentional, environmental, mechanical, electronic hardware, or software malfunctions. Are such risks justifiable under any circumstance? How can anyone justify the continuation of any kind of such weapons of mass destruction?

Greater emphasis must continue to me made in resolving world conflicts through negotiations by the United Nations Council, and other agencies around the world whose mission is to thwart aggression. Attainment of world peace must be every nation's purpose of governance, not aggression in solving conflicts.

The same concept of peace in families, churches, communities, places of employment, national states, and world regions must seek peaceful co-existence among its members.

In this day of internet commerce, it has been shown time after time, that criminal activities and security breaches occur widespread around the world. The control or ability of hacking to intercept and disrupt electronic commerce, power grids, air travel, banking, etc. is a viable deterrence in effecting control over rogue members of the worldwide community without resorting to violence and war with countries not abiding by international rules for peaceful coexistence.

Soldiers in wartime who in defending their nation or world peace, commits acts of war as part of their duty are not violating God's commandments, except for those who intentionally commit illegal acts of war for their own gratification. The judgment for acts of war atrocities falls on the souls of those who initiated the conflict. All countries should allow soldiers the right to serve in non-combat positions in support of self-defense efforts for reasons of conscientious objectors to combat roles.

DEATH PENALTY VS ATROCITIES OF WAR EUTHANAGIA/MERCY KILLING/SUICIDE

The most morally egregious acts against mankind and an offense against God the Creator is the destruction of life for whatever reasons. Life is precious from inception to death and under any circumstances should never be taken for granted, nor can it be justified as rational in times of war. Giving up one's life in order to protect another life is indeed an honorable action, but only as a last resort. Taking one's own life in order to avoid an agonizing death can never be justified.

Whoever would use capital punishment as the final means of deterrence should reevaluate the causes that influenced someone to kill someone else in a capital case trial. Other deterrents such as the use of medications causing either physical limitations or affecting mental judgment would eliminate the possibility of repeat offenses. This would be more acceptable than killing the offender. Medical or behavioral science may provide answers in helping develop alternatives in dealing with capital punishments as deterrence.

CHAPTER 19

POPE JOHN XXIV'S ADDRESS AT ATHENS OLYMPIC STATIUM IN ATHENS, GREECE ON OCTOBER 19, 2014 ON VATICAN TREASURES & LIBRARY

Matthew 25:14-30

"The Parable of the Talents. It will be as when a man who was going on a journey called in his servants and entrusted his possessions to them. To one he gave five talents; to another, two; to a third, one— to each according to his ability. Then he went away. Immediately the one who received five talents went and traded with them, and made another five. Likewise, the one who received two made another two. But the man who received one went off and dug a hole in the ground and buried his master's money. After a long time the master of those servants came back and settled accounts with them. The one who had received five talents came forward bringing the additional five. He said, 'Master, you gave me five talents. See, I have made five more.' His master said to him, 'Well done, my good and faithful servant. Since you were faithful in small matters, I will give you great responsibilities. Come, share your master's joy.' [Then] the one who had received two talents also came forward and said, 'Master, you gave me two talents. See, I have made two more.' His master said to him, 'Well done, my good and faithful servant. Since you were faithful in small matters, I will give you great responsibilities. Come,

share your master's joy.' Then the one who had received the one talent came forward and said, 'Master, I knew you were a demanding person, harvesting where you did not plant and gathering where you did not scatter; so out of fear I went off and buried your talent in the ground. Here it is back.' His master said to him in reply, 'You wicked, lazy servant! So you knew that I harvest where I did not plant and gather where I did not scatter? Should you not then have put my money in the bank so that I could have got it back with interest on my return? Now then! Take the talent from him and give it to the one with ten. For to everyone who has, more will be given and he will grow rich; but from the one who has not, even what he has will be taken away. And throw this useless servant into the darkness outside, where there will be wailing and grinding of teeth.' "[5]

The "treasures" in the Vatican Library and other storage facilities for amassing the gifts of God to humanity is very much like the servant who buried his master's property that had been entrusted to him. Are we not as guilty? These treasures need to be preserved and protected for posterity by others, but whose function is it to preserve these past treasures, for they must be shared with the world. Entities in the world have the resources and capacities needed to maintain, catalogue, and archive through internet resources, so all can enjoy and benefit, including providing resulting resources to benefit the poor, and afflicted. It is not just for the Pope, or a few scholars or researchers to peruse. We must use all our talents and resources for doing God's work throughout the world. This is one of Jesus' most important teachings that we have been entrusted to pass on to the world. How can we ask of them what we ourselves are failing to do?

We should not be in the business of being archivist or maintaining museums, our mission by Christ has been to proclaim the word of God, to shepherd My flock, and to feed My sheep. I am directing that we put up all the contents of our museums and libraries for auction starting immediately. How can we justify holding these treasures when the world poor have no food or shelters for their families? We will utilize that money to spearhead worldwide programs, in cooperation with others, whose programs are to eradicate hunger by helping countries to grow their own food, and create the means to irrigate barren lands to be productive for sustainability. It is not productive just to feed people, but we must empower them to be self-supporting so that hunger can be eliminated. Education must also be a part of economic sustainability of their lives and for their families, and eliminate the endless cycle of welfare from which they have no ability alone to escape. No society should seek to cast its members in accordance to rank or class, the haves and the have not's. Those are not just societies, whose sole purpose is greed and self-aggrandizement.   We will lead by example, not by supporting coercive governments who do not provide for their people. We are brothers and sisters in Christ, and it is our responsibility to share with others our bountiful harvest, our blessings, and riches. Our Lord is not seeking us to glorify Him and Our Father in creating magnificent luxurious edifices, but to do His mission on earth. No longer will the episcopacy of our church live lives more affluent than of that of their congregations. The sins of the episcopacy of the church has for too long in history held itself to be on a pedestal, above common man in stature and deserving to be treated like nobility. Christ himself has taught us that the last shall be first and first shall be last, and that the teacher is to be the servant of others. It is time that the episcopacy of the church leads by example as Christ has asked of us. How can we truly lead the church into the final era of Christ's mission in the world, if we in the episcopacy don't practice what we preach to His followers?

CHAPTER 20

ATTEMPT ON POPE JOHN XXIV'S LIFE

September 22, 2014 at Salt Lake Stadium, Kolkata, India, it is expected that an estimated crowd of one million will be in the stands and fields in order to participate in the Pope's visit. The preparation has been unprecedented for the organizers to make this event run efficiently, including the massive security precautions for the Pontiff's visit. Thousands of vendors have been enlisted to help provide food, beverages, and sanitation facilities required for this event. If the Pontiff's past appearances at announced worldwide stadiums are any indications, the local resources will be totally maxed out.

There have been repeated reports of anti-Pope violent protest demonstrations groups including an escalation of death threats as the scheduled event nears. It has been reported, that the Pontiff has pleaded that if any attempts are made, only be on his life and not on the masses of people who are coming to these events. He is undaunted by his mission to attend these planned events.

The Pope's airplane departed Rome and is on its way to India for a planned three day schedule of private and group meetings with various non-Catholic religious leaders from the entire region, who have asked for inclusion in the Pontiff's itinerary.

If previous excursions by the Pontiff are any indications, the meetings have produced a flurry of extended communications among religious denominations with the Holy See in Rome, and unprecedented unification talks. It thus would appear that the Pontiff's push for unification is taking the world religions by hurricane forces. Everyone seems on fire whether for or against, but it would appear that unification efforts are making major strides.

On the Pope's plane everyone is multitasking in order to ensure that the Pontiff's scheduled itinerary is confirmed. Biographical and thematic briefs are being prepared for the Pontiff on the various individuals and groups that are to meet with him in order to maximize the effectiveness of intended dialogs that are to be discussed within allotted times.

All of a sudden, the plane inexplicably surges upward similar to a rocket lifting for a space flight, with huge flares propelled from the rear and under the aircraft, going in various directions. The oxygen masks quickly fall above the passengers, as instructions blare from the speakers for everyone to buckle up for evasive procedures. Everyone is cringing to glimpse out the windows to see what is going on. In the distance below them, they now see multiple explosions in rapid succession, causing the aircraft to vibrate violently in various directions with each explosion.

The pilot quickly comes on the radio. "Please be assured, we are now safe, with no damage to the aircraft, and will be able to land safely at our destination. We have reported the surface to air missiles strikes to the military, and they have launched fast response teams to deal with the situation. "Please be assured that I am a veteran combat pilot and the aircraft was purchased from the President of The United States, who is committed to keeping the Pontiff safe. This is a very sophisticated and capable plane. We are now at cruising altitude, and will have a calm flight till we reach our destination. I apologize for your discomfort and turbulence. The flight staff will help to restore the cabin to preflight conditions, and have available clothing to change if required. Thank you for your understanding."

Although the inside of the plane was in a disheveled state, no injuries were reported; the staff was quick to respond to everyone's needs and calm restored among the passengers, including the Pope. The Pope then spoke over the speaker system. "My dear staff, I also apologize for the scare, but I could not warn you ahead of the potential threats on my life and to those of you within my entourage. But I had been warned by Jesus, that these things would occur and not to worry, that I would be safe till he calls me to my eternal rest. In that, I also assumed that His protection would extend to you also. So rest assured we are indeed in the palm of His hands. Please rest comfortably for the remainder of the flight, giving thanks to Our Lord for our safety and the work ahead of us in India.

Thanks be to God!"

Upon arriving and meeting the crowd at the airport, the Pope is asked if he had a good flight. His response was, "Yes indeed, this is an amazing aircraft, and it was like being in the palms of the hands of The Lord Jesus himself, Amen."

CHAPTER 21

POPE JOHN XXIV'S ADDRESS AT ABJUJA STADIUM IN ABUJA, NIGERIA

PURGATORY

There has been much written about whether "purgatory" exist. Many believe that since the bible does not mention the word purgatory that it does not therefor exist. Many only believed that at death only hell and heaven existed. Thus souls in "limbo" or awaiting the opening of the gates of heaven were in hell.

The subject of purgatory has been exhaustively been written about over the centuries, but a very authoritative book should be utilized for an in depth understanding of critical thinking on this subject. I will be quoting from this document. "The Hope of Eternal Life", was developed as a resource by the Committee for Ecumenical and Interreligious

Affairs of the United States Conference of Catholic Bishops (USCCB) and the Ecumenical and Inter-Religious Relations section of the Evangelical Lutheran Church in America (ELCA). Copyright C 2011 by Lutheran University Press, the Evangelical Lutheran Church in America, and the United States Conference of Catholic Bishops

"If we die still deformed by sin, but will finally live before God fully transformed into what God intends for humanity, then some sort of change or transformation must occur between death and entry into eschatological glory. In this sense, the general topic of "purgation" is unavoidable. What is the nature of this transformation?

In Matthew 12:32, where Jesus says: "Whoever speaks a word against the Son of Man will be forgiven, but whoever speaks against the Holy Spirit will not be forgiven, either in this age or in the age to come. That the sin against the Holy Spirit will not be forgiven in the age to come sometimes has been interpreted to mean that there are other sins that can be forgiven in the world to come, that is, in purgatory.

Augustine, substantially contributed to the development of the doctrine of purgatory. His *City of God*, especially its last three books (20-22) addresses the final judgment, punishment, and heaven. These works became the source *par excellence* for later Western eschatology. In Book 21, he asks whether divine punishment beyond death is strictly retributive, the just consequence of earlier sin, or also purgative and remedial. A remedial punishment would clearly end if and when it brings about its intended improvement. Some punishments within this life are remedial. Augustine believes the same is true of some post-death punishment. He states, "Not all who suffer temporal punishment after death are doomed to the eternal pains that follow the last judgment. For, as I have said, what is not forgiven in this life is pardoned in the life to come, in the case of those who are not to suffer eternal punishment."

Pope Benedict XVI, in his encyclical on hope, *Spe salvi*, describes this fire as Christ in a passage that deserves to be quoted at length:

"Some recent theologians are of the opinion that the fire which both burns and saves. Is Christ himself, the Judge and Saviour. The encounter with him is the decisive act of judgment. Before his gaze all falsehood melts away. This encounter with him, as it burns us, transforms and frees us, allowing us to become truly ourselves. All that we build during our lives can prove to be mere straw, pure bluster, and it collapses. Yet in the pain of this encounter, when the impurity and sickness of our lives become evident to us, there lies salvation. His gaze, the touch of his heart heals us through an undeniably painful transformation "as through fire". But it is a blessed pain, in which the holy power of his love sears through us like a flame, enabling us to become totally ourselves and thus totally of God. In this way the inter-relation between justice and grace also becomes clear: the way we live our lives is not immaterial, but our defilement does not stain us forever if we have at least continued to reach out towards Christ, towards truth and towards love. Indeed, it has already been burned away through Christ's Passion. At the moment of judgment we experience and we absorb the overwhelming power of his love over all the evil in the world and in ourselves. The pain of love becomes our salvation and our joy."

This teaching makes clear that the Catholic doctrine of purgatory and the Lutheran teaching of the self being purified by death-and-resurrection intend to describe the same reality - namely, the process by which the self, distracted during this life by sin and the remnants of sin, is turned fully to Christ, purified of all that would hinder perfect communion with God, Christ, and the saints that will be the life of heaven. Expiation for residual effects of the consequences for sinful acts emphasize our personal responsibility for sin and are contextualized and integrated within a more comprehensive picture of the power of God's love to transform the justified into persons fit for the kingdom.

As Ratzinger stated: "Purgatory is not, as Tertullian thought, some kind of supraworldly concentration camp where man is forced to undergo punishment in a more or less arbitrary fashion. Rather is it the inwardly necessary process of transformation in which a person becomes capable of Christ, capable of God and thus capable of unity with the whole communion of saints."

3) *A greater integration of purgation with death and judgment.*
The images of purgatorial fire as Christ symbolizes the integration of purgatory with judgment itself. The encounter with Christ as Judge is the moment of purification. Must this purification be interpreted as temporally extended in time? "Time" in this context must be understood analogously. Pope Benedict XVI explains: "It is clear that we cannot calculate the 'duration' of this transforming burning in terms of the chronological measurements of this world. The transforming 'moment' of this encounter eludes earthly time-reckoning-it is the heart's time, it is the time of 'passage' to communion with God in the Body of Christ." Karl Rahner, while

granting that this purification is a process (i.e., every aspect of the person is perhaps not transformed simultaneously), nevertheless sought to incorporate purification as a moment within the entire event of death as a closing of life and a confrontation with God. If purification works within the person, cleansing the self in accord with the self's nature, then it perhaps must have a certain extension or "duration," but the temporal categories for understanding that extension must be applied with restraint, as was explicitly stated by the Congregation for Divine Worship and the Discipline of the Sacraments in its 2001 *Directory on Popular Piety and the Liturgy*.

4) *A specification of the ecumenically necessary.*
Recent discussions of purgatory have stressed the bond of love that unites the living and the departed, a unity expressed in an unbroken community of prayer. In *Spe salvi*, Benedict acknowledged that while the Orthodox do "not recognize the purifying and expiatory suffering of souls in the afterlife," they do share with the Catholic Church the practice of praying for the departed. In his earlier book on *Eschatology*, he had affirmed in relation to the Catholic-Orthodox disagreement on purgatory: "What is primary is the praxis of being able to pray, and being called upon to pray. The objective correlate of this praxis in the world to come need not, in some reunification of the churches, be determined of necessity in a strictly unitary fashion. . . ."

While such a common basis in practice does not exist between Catholics and Lutherans, the openness to a variety of conceptualizations of the state of those who die in need of further purification is important.

Agreements:

Catholics and Lutherans agree:

1.   During this life, the justified "are not exempt from a lifelong struggle against the contradiction to God within the selfish desires of the old Adam (see Gal. 5:16; Rom. 7:7-10)" (JDDJ, 28; cf. Trent DS 1515 and 1690 and LC, Baptism, paras. 6567).

2.   This struggle is rightly described by a variety of categories: e.g., penitence, healing, daily dying and rising with Christ.

3.   Borne in Christ, the painful aspects of this struggle are a participation in Christ's suffering and death. Catholic teachings call these pains temporal punishments; the Lutheran Confessions grant they can, "in a formal sense," be called punishments.

4.   This ongoing struggle does not indicate an insufficiency in Christ's saving work, but is an aspect of our being conformed to Christ and his saving work.

5.   The effects of sin in the justified are fully removed only as they die, undergo judgment, and encounter the purifying love of Christ. The justified are transformed from their condition at death to the condition with which they will be blessed in eternal glory. All, even martyrs and saints of the highest order, will find the encounter with

the Risen Christ transformative in ways beyond human comprehension.

6.   Christ transforms those who enter into eternal life. This change is a work of God's grace. It can be rightly understood as our final and perfect transformation by Christ (Phil 3:21). The fire of Christ's love burns away all that is incompatible with living in the direct presence of God. It is the complete death of the old person, leaving only the new person in Christ.

7.   Scripture tells us little about the process of the transformation from this life to entrance into eternal life. Categories of space and time can be applied only analogously.

Distinctive Teachings
Catholics are committed to the doctrine of purgatory, i.e., to a process of purgation that occurs in or after death, and to the possibility that the living by their prayers can aid the departed undergoing this process. This aid will be discussed in the next section of this treatise, but here it should be noted that, for Catholic teaching, purgatory must be so understood as not to exclude this possibility. As the survey of Catholic teaching on purgatory above shows, there is no binding Catholic doctrine on the spatial or temporal character of purgatory, on how many Christians go through purgatory, or on the intensity or extent of their sufferings. While all the justified are transformed by eternal glory, Catholics admit the

possibility that some people incur no further punishment after death.

Lutherans teach that all the justified remain sinners unto death. Sin and the effects of sin in those who die in Christ will be removed prior to entrance into eternal glory. In effect, they teach the reality of purgation, even if not as a distinct intermediate state. The rejection by the Lutheran Reformers of the doctrine of purgatory as they knew it focused on practices and abuses perceived as bound up with this teaching. They judged that the doctrine of purgatory obscured the gospel of free grace. The Lutheran Confessions explicitly express a willingness to discuss purgatory if the doctrine were separated from these practices and abuses, although at the same time expressing doubt about the biblical foundation of any such teaching.

The differences between Catholic and Lutheran teaching on purgatory thus focus on 1) how the living relate to those undergoing this purgation, and 2) the extent and explicit character of the binding teaching on purgation and purgatory. The more explicit the binding teaching, the greater the difficulty Lutherans have in seeing this teaching as biblical and thus binding. We have seen in this dialogue that explicit Catholic doctrine on purgatory is more limited than often recognized. As the Catholic attitude toward differences with the Orthodox indicates, these two differences are not entirely separable. Common practices toward the dead can provide an assurance that permits diversity in formulation. The following discussion of prayer for the dead must thus be considered in assessing the ecumenical significance of Catholic-Lutheran understandings of purgatory.

Convergences
Today, Lutheran and Catholic teaching integrates purgation with death, judgment, and the encounter with Christ. Recent Catholic and Lutheran understandings of purgation sound remarkably similar. While the word "purgatory" remains an ecumenically charged term, and for many Catholics and Lutherans signals a sharp division, our work in this round has shown that our churches' understandings of how the justified enter eternal glory are closer than expected.

In light of the analysis given above, this dialogue believes that the topic of purgation, in and of itself, need not divide our communions."[6]

As can be seen from the dialogue between the Catholic and Lutherans in this book, finding common acceptance on the existence of purgatory has not been resolved. It is therefore important that the theology of purgatory be regarded as part of the Catholic Doctrine with the appropriate understanding for those who are to become members of the Universal Catholic Church. Each of the various Christian denominations has their own interpretation of this theology, and therefore in order to be one with the Catholic Church, it must be reconciled. It must be accepted as part of the universal Catholic doctrine.

When we remember the parable of the workers in the vineyard who were paid the same regardless of the length of time they had actually worked, we have a glimpse of the mercy and love of our heavenly Father. If we also consider the premise given on the subject of God's judgement and it's transformative healing power of the soul in HIS presence that time in purgatory cannot be measured in human understanding.

When Christ appeared to us recently, He provided for us the knowledge of what purgatory is and how the soul is to be purified until it can be accepted into its heavenly reward. We therefore have His own explanation as to the existence of purgatory.

SACRAMENT OF RECONCILIATION

Jesus also instituted the Sacrament of Reconciliation so that all those living would have the means, by which all who believed in Him, could reconcile the state of their souls with that of His glorified existence. Because of man's free will and the continued existence of evil influences in the world, our souls continually need cleansing till our hour of death, when we shall all be judged. When Christ died upon the cross, it opened the gates of heaven for all who had died previously in "limbo", and for those after the resurrection whose souls shall have been judge purified. Saint Thomas Aquinas: "The words of The Lord (This day....in paradise) must therefore be understood not of an earthly or corporeal paradise, but of that spiritual paradise in which all may be, said to be, who are in the enjoyment of the divine glory. Hence, the thief went up with Christ to heaven that he might be with Christ, as it was said to him: "Thou shalt be with Me in Paradise"; but as to reward, he was in Paradise, for he there tasted and enjoyed the divinity of Christ, together with the other saints."[3][4][5][7]

Jesus therefore was proclaiming that the gates of heaven, which had been closed since the original sin of Adam & Eve, as promised by HIS Father, would be open upon His resurrection. Jesus was not proclaiming that all future sins were forgiven, that is why he created the Sacrament of Reconciliation. As the thief who died on Calvary on that day, and for all those whose sins have been forgiven through reconciliation and remain in a state of grace, or through the anointing of the sick, which includes the forgiveness of their sins, shall go directly to their heavenly reward at the time of their deaths. They will not return for the "last judgment", since they have already earned eternity with GOD.

Much has been written and interpreted about the end times and the last judgment, which is to occur. It will occur only after the final era of the Lord, for those who still exist at that time, and for the souls still in purgatory. Those who upon their death entered directly into hell have already been judged for eternity. They will not be judged again at the final last judgment.

Now is the time for the final era of the Lord to begin. And that is what the Lord Jesus is asking us to do. We must work diligently to achieve the unification of all who believe in God into one Universal

Catholic Church Family. The daunting task of unification is the standard by which all those who are living will be judged at the time of their death.

For those of us, whose time will come, at God's choosing, we will have our final judgment based on how we responded to his call for living as disciples and our efforts in bringing about unification. This is not a whimsical order from anyone. For we have heard our Lord Jesus Himself make this request. Will our remaining life's work be reflected in actions that truly demonstrate our commitment to the beliefs of our faith, our own families, our work, our church, our community, our nations, and in the world we live in?

For various religions around the world, including the Catholic Church, who relish their own individual identities and whose religious beliefs are centered on self-glorification and not on the Commandments and the teachings our Lord Jesus Christ, they will need to change in order that unification of a Universal Catholic Church can be achieved.

The Commandments and the teachings of our Lord Jesus Christ will have to be the central faith doctrines for discussions in the unifications of all Christian churches. All church doctrines, regulatory guidelines, and operational guidelines will need to be revised in order for the Universal Catholic Church to be inclusive rather than exclusive.

We are to be a Universal Catholic Church Family, in beliefs, actions, and committed to each other. We must live as the Lord taught us in his prayer of the "Our Father" teaching us about forgiveness, treating each other with love, and compassion. We cannot be an island onto ourselves. We must treat each other as brothers and sisters as part of Christ's body; we are our brothers and sisters keeper.

Our work is to unify all Christian churches around the world into one body. It is God's belief that by our example, not by aggressive methods of control, we will influence the people of the world to emulate the peacefulness of our united existence, in love, acceptance, and charitable co-existence. In doing so, we can bring about a peaceful existence for all inhabitants of mother earth, a world without the threat of wars or hunger. A world that can utilize money previously spent on military superiority or defense, on recovery of disasters, curing diseases, cancer, helping to change the cycles of human indignities and diseases affecting the lives of people living on the fringes of society, cleaning our environment, and providing new sources of food and energies.

Christ himself has returned to ask us to take on this endeavor. The Catholic Church Episcopacy has previously failed so far in its obligation to evangelize to the extent desired by GOD the Father. It will take each and every one of us to become Disciples of Christ to achieve this undertaking. We are his workers in the vineyard for generations that will follow us. BE A DISCIPLE OF CHRIST

I bless you in the Name of the Father, The Son, and the Holy Spirit." Pope John XXIV

CHAPTER 22

VATICAN CONSPIRATORS

The "gang of 5" Cardinals' Thrombus, Rossini, Pompus, Kroni, and Bambu, are meeting at an undisclosed location away from St Peters in order to plan for their latest attempt at killing the Pope. They are now getting desperate after all the failed attempts to stop the Pope from embarking on worldwide reconciliation with religious leaders to formalize a Universal Catholic Church. Various ethnic groups, who oppose these efforts from Rome, have been trying to derail talks with protest demonstrations and every conceivable obstructive ploy to prevent unification. But somehow the talks are continuing, and seem to be unstoppable.

"Cardinal Rossini, when are we going to start getting results from these attempts, it is getting more difficult to meet and plan?" "Dear Cardinal Pompus, I wholly understand your frustrations, as we all are, but this time we are taking the gloves off to make sure it gets done once and for all. I have asked Giovanni Jesuppi from the Sicilian mob to plan an extreme terrorist type of attack on the Pope. We have no choice now, since every inconspicuous attempt has failed so far."

"Giovanni wants a $5 million dollars upfront payment before he proceeds with this plan." 'That's a lot of money Cardinal Rossini,' pipes up Cardinal Bambu. 'How can we be sure that it's going to work this time?' "Well he has briefly laid out the plan, which requires a lot of surveillance on our part since we are the only ones who can get close to the Pope without raising suspicion. We need to get specific timing and schedules of the Pope's upcoming appointments and daily routines, so that we can be as precise as to his whereabouts at all times within his apartment, and offices." 'You mean Cardinal Rossini that they will strike inside of St. Peters?' said Cardinal Kroni. "Yes, if we are to succeed and derail the Pope's efforts at unification, we must have a catastrophic event that will scare everyone from wanting to join in this effort. It will produce fear and destabilize the current undertakings by the Church. It will mean a great deal of casualties, but that is the price of war." 'But what about us?' ask Cardinal Thrombus. "We will be told of the timing so that we can be away at the time of the attack. I assure you." says Cardinal Rossini.

"So the first order of business is I need a million dollars in cash from each of you by tomorrow noon. Then I'll bring the money to Giovanni to put the plan in motion. The next thing I'll need from you is to notate every minute of the Pope's routine schedule for the next two weeks. I can get the Pope's schedule for the next month from his secretary, and I'll coordinate all that data for Giovanni so they can plan out an attack. Remember to keep secret your activities so no one suspects your purpose. Straddle your timing of the Pope's surveillance, as well as the containers of cash that you bring to me, to make sure you are not seen."

Cardinal Rossini travels by car the next evening for a planned rendezvous with Giovanni. In a parking garage, their cars are parked alongside next to each other, driver to driver. Their windows slowly open, and Cardinal Rossini starts passing the bags of money, and a schematic of the architectural details of the papal apartment and offices, to Giovanni. "I assume Cardinal Rossini; I don't need to count the money since you are a priest." 'Yes, yes be assured Giovanni. You can start preparations and in two weeks I'll have the Pope's schedule for you as you have asked. I'll give you a call when to meet.' Slowly the cars pull out of their parking spaces, and disappear into the darkness without their lights on, using night goggle vision gear.

Two weeks later the same scenario occurs at the garage with the passing of the Pope's itinerary followed by the cars disappearing in the night.

A month later, Cardinal Rossini gets a cell call. Just the words "June 5, 2:10 p.m.", and a hang up. Quickly Cardinal Rossini sends a text message to the other Cardinals. In his mind, he notes to himself. It is set.

On a sunny afternoon, traffic is moving along Rome's streets and the plaza's leading to St. Peter's Square. Noticeable diagonally on the left side across the plaza from the Pope's apartment, construction vehicles are parked. Workmen with tools are milling about setting up cautionary signs for people to avoid the area. At precisely 2:09 p.m., side doors on the van open quickly, a major flash appears from the doors, and a surface to air missile is seen to head straight toward the Pope's apartment. And just as quickly, a huge cylindrical radiant bright yellow shield appears just in front of the Pope's apartment. The surface to air missile hits the shield and mysteriously disappears. One of the assailant, cries out "Mama Mia, this Pope truly is protected, let's get out of here!" Hurriedly the assailant's vehicle screeches out of the plaza, leaving behind everything they had set up to distract the crowds. Sirens start to blare as the crowds quickly seek shelter in the buildings around the plaza.

The Vatican guards are rushing to the scene as well as the police from the city.

Hundreds of cars, fire trucks, rescue vehicles and a swat team pour into the plaza. Everyone from those vehicles, have guns drawn and searching around the plaza. The head of the swat team blares out commands for the various groups to mobilize for finding any evidence left behind by the terrorists and to interrogate any witnesses. He calls on the Vatican guards to quickly have their security camera feeds transmitted to the swat command vehicle immediately.

Reporters and their staff are also pouring around the square, which has been cordoned off by the police to keep spectators from compromising the crime scene. TV and radio satellites are everywhere in the distance. Reporters are pressing the police to give them any bits of information so they can run a story. But as the scramble is on, various conspiracies are being speculated as to what type of terrorist attack occurred on the Pope's life are now being transmitted all over the world on radios and TV news reports, in an attempt to be first to put out a story.

In the Papal apartment, Vatican guards and security forces have invaded the Pope's chambers. But the Pope remains calm throughout the events and asks the head of security to please ask his men to pull back from the apartment and his offices, so that he can resume his schedule. The Pope says, "As you can see I am perfectly fine, and as I was told by our Lord, that no harm would come to me, so you can be assured that I'm in good hands." The head of security than ask his staff to return to their post. Pope John XXIV then turns and heads into his private chapel for a prayer of thanksgiving.

In their haste to leave, the assailants left all kinds of evidence at their assault location, in particular when they screeched out with their van doors still open, materials fell out from the van. The swat team called in a mobile forensic lab to start examining every shred of evidence they have uncovered. It will be hours if not days before they determine who was behind the attack, especially since no group has come forward to claim responsibility for the failed attack.

The "gang of five", are now communicating what they are hearing of the failed attack through the various news stories. Some are getting very nervous that they could be implicated, and are now talking about resigning and disappearing for a while. The miracle story of the huge disk appearing that swallowed up the missile has truly frazzled them. Knowing that the Pope is truly being protected, they therefore conclude that there is no way any attempts on the Pope's life can be successful. They all decide it is now time to leave, but to make sure they give various reasons for resigning, so not to give reason to speculate about their sinister involvement.

CHAPTER 23

POPE JOHN XXIV'S ADDRESS AT MICHIGAN STADIUM, ANN HARBOR, MICHIGAN USA SEPTEMBER 4, 2014

CONTROVERSIES

"American Catholics, for their part, believe it much less important to adhere to strict Catholic teachings, prompting some theologians to refer to their mind-set as "cafeteria style catholic" picking and choosing what they liked. The independence of the Catholic laity as they became more educated, wealthier, and worldly increased the opportunities for friction between them and the traditional hierarchy."[8]

European and Canadian Catholics believe even more than Americans in being intellectually independent from Catholic teachings. A very glaring example is the percentage attending church services in those regions. Compared to these groups, Americans are actually courted heavily by the Pope and Curia because they believe that they will fall in line with their teachings or directives at a higher percentage than any other foreign group. Good examples are the following:

1. Most liturgical changes have occurred in the United States, such as the recent changes demanded by the Roman Liturgical office to return to language in the liturgy that was pre-Vatican Council, because they said that the restored language more correctly reflects the original Latin translation. (I.e. the word

Consubstantiation restored within the context of the Creed had not been used since the translation changes at the time of the Vatican Council in 1963-64. So the conservatives within the church are showing their power.) These changes were made through the American Church because they believed that they were the easiest National Bishops Conference to influence. By getting them to change, then all the other National Bishops Conferences in other countries would follow in line.

2.   The changes in the organizational structure of Catholic Seminaries and adherence to traditional orthodoxy of theological, scriptural and moral teachings were demanded by Rome of the American Church, before any other National Church Conference. Belief—change America and everyone else will follow.

3.   The development of the new American Catholic Catechism was required by Rome to be revised and with final approval by Rome promulgated. Only then were other National Conferences required to develop their own.

The American Catholic Church provides the highest level of income to support Rome than any other combined donations from other National Conferences. Rome still believes that they can control the American Church from following the pattern of other National Churches in staying true to a traditional conservative church.

POLITICS

Matthew 22:21[9] Jesus said "Repay to Caesar what belongs to Caesar and to God what belongs to God." This quote has guided me throughout my life in considering conflicting moral choices dealing with questions between Church and State issues. When you really reflect on the teachings proclaimed by Jesus, we have the ability to make better informed choices.

Today with clearer understanding and better perspective, we can look at historical conflicts between secular societies and church authority and question the legitimacy of events such as the numerous Crusades to win back the Holy Lands from the "Infidels". Historically the church was silent in confronting Hitler's takeover of the European continent, its silence to the issue of apartheid societies like in South Africa, or condoning the issue of slavery by the American Churches by supporting separate churches for blacks and whites in the Southern States of the United States. The church cannot impose its beliefs on the unbelievers in this world.

But we need to educate and impart on our followers the legitimacy and validity of doctrines and principles of the Catholic Church. It is by the example of how we live our lives, that we can truly inspire others to want to enrich their lives by our practices. It is not by demanding allegiance and adherence to our beliefs through force or coercion that we instill our values in others. God has given us free will; non-Catholics have a right to their beliefs.

We need to be conscious of criticism against the Church for events that presented a conflicting or inconsistent view of the Lord's teachings. On one trip to South America, Pope John Paul was seen scolding a kneeling priest who had been involved with groups seeking the overthrow of a corrupt government. The Pope demanded that the priest repent of his involvement and to keep faithful to his priestly responsibilities. And yet at another time, John Paul II seemed to show a blind or benevolent eye towards the large number of priests involved in Poland, who actively supported or lead "Solidarity" groups throughout the country. There was even some limited sabotage activities against companies supported by the government, even though "Solidarity" groups were generally pacifists. "The Catholic Church had been no stranger to the political arena; in 1980 the Vatican decreed that no priest or nun could hold a public office in the government. This decree was specifically aimed at the rebellious, liberal priest and U.S. Congress member from Massachusetts, Father Robert Drinan, forcing him to resign his seat in May 1980, but the larger implication of the decree resonated throughout the period. The Vatican was taking a hardline stance against liberal radical priests and nuns, who veered away from traditional church teachings. Drinan, in his ten years in the House of Representatives, often voted for abortion rights, an act that infuriated the Vatican and conservative Catholics everywhere. The anti- politics decree served the Vatican greatly in disciplining several nuns who joined campaigns for women's rights and abortion rights. Sister Agnes Mary Mansour, acting director of the Michigan Department of Social Services and a nun in the Sisters of Mercy of the Union Order for thirty years, was ordered by the Vatican in 1983 to step down from her position in social services or to resign as a nun. The controversy surrounding Mansour involved the issue of the social-services department she worked for administering public funds for abortions. Mansour, though personally opposed to abortions, felt that her position in government was helping many people, and that the Catholic Church was doing a disservice to women. Therefore, she abandoned her vocation as a nun. Similarly Sisters Elizabeth Morancy and Arlene Violet were forced out of the Sisters of Mercy Community, after they were elected to public office in Rhode Island. Several other clergy members and Catholic organizations, such as the National Coalition of American Nuns and Catholics for a Free Choice, clashed with the Vatican on this ban, seeing it as skewed toward only liberal groups, while conservative cardinals, priests, and bishops were given free rein to state publicly their staunch opposition to issues such as abortion, gay rights and the candidates that supported them."[10]

SEPARATION OF CHURCH AND STATE

Politics of the established episcopacy has involved a battle of orthodox conservative traditions verses modernity or the evolved enlightenment of the laity. To hold onto traditions in order to justify the status quo on celibacy, sexuality, science, modern uses of communications, political differences, and confronting and dealing with realities of life is nothing more than self-serving ideologies.

The ban on priest or nuns from holding political office was previously instituted to control them from giving the allusion of Church involvement in political debates and influencing voting on individual's issues in conflict with Church doctrines and supposed ethical conflicts between Church and State. It now currently exists, although not as a ban, but by publically expressing to all members of the Catholic Church critical vilifying statements about public officials who are exercising their rights to disagree with Church positions either as politicians or supporters.

Jesus was asked the following question. Knowing their malice, Jesus said, "Why are you testing me, you hypocrites? Show me the coin that pays the census tax." Then they handed him the Roman coin, and he said to them, "Whose image is this and whose inscription?"

They replied, "Caesar's."

Then he said to them, "Then repay to Caesar what belongs to Caesar, and to God what belongs to God."[11]

Jesus' answer has been my guiding principle in dealing with political quandaries that we experience in our daily lives. In the Constitution of the United States of America, Americans are granted freedom of religious expression. That religious freedom enjoins the responsibility that others also have the right of freedom from religious intolerance. In essence we cannot impose our religious beliefs on others. We can express our opinions and help to encourage or persuade others, but it should never be done in any manner that vilifies or threatens physical or psychological harm to others. Our strongest strength is in exercising our right to vote and allow our democratic process to work.

The old adage "never talk about politics if you want to remain friends" has always been true from the earliest of times. However, it is a subject that truly needs to be addressed by the church in order to give guidance to its members.

When the late Senator Ted Kennedy was allowed to have a Catholic mass for his funeral, some individuals became very belligerent in their disapproval because of his stance on abortion rights and therefore claiming he did not deserve one. This illustrates a simple example of militant intolerance of individuals who maintain a strict adherence to traditions of orthodox principles. In simpler terms, "Black is Black, and White is White, there are no Greys". Well in reality, there are greys. Jesus taught us to be loving and forgiving, even of our enemies. We are all sinners. Should a single sin, be the sole measure of a man? Should that be the basis of whether we vote against a politician? Unfortunately that is how many people vote. Do we want God to decide where we go for eternity based on a single sin?

We have seen throughout the existing world nations and their past violent histories plagued by ethnic wars as a result of greed, nationalistic aspiration, and even religious intolerances. Have we not learned from these histories, that trying to impose one's religious beliefs on others, is trying to infringe on the rights of others. We must learn to lead by example. Our faith beliefs and how we live our lives must be the proof of the happiness that our faith embellishes upon our spirit, so that others may want to emulate. That is the power of our faith without coercion, vilification, or militant tactics that abuse the very persons we would want to encourage accepting our faith beliefs.

Violent confrontation on whatever issues that plague a supposedly civilized world has never been effective in resolving the problems of any country or regional conflict. Civil discourse and mediation either by legislative or judicial action have been the only courageous way to resolve combative issues. The ability to change and willingness to accept a compromise as a viable solution is further required to actually implement the steps necessary for resolution.

Passionate debate of issues must be tempered with discovering the appropriate actions necessary to achieve the desired result. In the past the church allowed peoples passions on issues to inflame prejudicial opinions surrounding conflict about the teachings of Jesus. People not treated with respect and compassion often resulted in them leaving the church because of maltreatment or alienation. Further, in issues dealing with curtailment of religious rights vs. civil rights, the churches actions elicited public outcries that tended to inflame public opinions against the church. The issues of non-tolerance of church involvement in civil activities, including the non-allowance of public prayer in schools, and the removal of displays of religious monuments in public places were the result of legal proceedings. The only way the church will be able to achieve success in these matters will be to promote legislative enactments of laws which would grant those rights. The visceral attacks by people and the church only amplify the disparities of Church vs. State. The primary driving force of the laws under the US Constitution has been the protection of the rights of the individual against oppressions. Until the Catholic Church accepts that people will not tolerate religion being force upon them, the constitution will not be changed to tolerate religious freedom. We must work to protect guaranteed religious freedoms in our church facilities; otherwise we risk the abrogation of all our freedoms.

These limitations on religious rights were often the result of lawsuits brought by atheists through the ACLU.

ABORTION, EUTHANASIA, MERCY KILLING

"The issue of abortion has been at the forefront of much of the heated debate that occurs between liberal Catholics and more traditional ones. American Catholics for the most part believe that abortion is wrong, but few believe it to be a mortal sin, an act of murder. Some Catholics believe that issues of contraception, abortion, and sexuality are personal matters that could be handled without the church interference. Many Catholics regarded the encyclical *Humane Vitae* (1968), the Vatican's doctrine on sexuality and contraception, as too intrusive, and Pope John Paul II's desire to enforce it too draconian. Father Charles E. Curran, a Catholic theologian at Catholic University in Washington,

D.C., had his teaching license revoked in 1986 by Joseph Cardinal Ratzinger, head of the Vatican's Congregation for the Doctrine of the Faith, for preaching against the Vatican's official teachings on sexuality and abortion. Curran's dismissal served as a warning to church officials to abide by official teachings or be severely reprimanded. The Vatican has labeled abortion an unspeakable crime, and therefore church leaders are urged to act against it. Newly appointed cardinals, such as Bernard Law of Boston and John O'Connor of New York placed the issue on the forefront of the Catholic agenda in 1984. O'Connor, who labeled the issue his "No. 1 priority," compared abortion to the Holocaust and directly criticized Democratic vice presidential candidate Geraldine Ferraro, a Catholic, for her prochoice position. This direct reference to politics and highly visible political figure caused Mario Cuomo, the governor of New York and also a prochoice Catholic, to enter the debate and defend a Catholic's right to choose without compromising her church membership. The church remained unyielding in its belief in a pro-life stance, so much so that in 1985 the National Conference of Catholic Bishops updated the ten-year-old prolife document "Pastoral Plan for Pro-Life Activities: A Reaffirmation." The issue struck a chord with Catholic women and nuns, many of whom viewed the question of this debate as a woman's right to decide the fate of her own body and not a decision that should be made by a male-dominated church. Activist nuns, such as Sister Traxler, a member of the School Sisters of Notre Dame for more than forty years, saw the issue of abortion as the most prominent example of the church's debasement of women, The National Coalition of American Nuns helped to sponsor a pro-choice advertisement in 1984 to counterattack the harassment they felt that women were receiving from an overbearing Vatican. The strong, rebellious stance of female religious symbolized the rift that was developing in the church because of perceived sexism."

The Church must require that pro-life not be an issue regarding whether or not a woman has the right to decide the fate of their bodies, but that the Church must declare it is pro-life for the continued life of a fetus. The existence of life is sacred with a soul. The Holy Spirit dwells within the soul until natural life ends. Therefore the debate about mercy killing, euthanasia, and abortion regards the defense of the existence of the soul. God extends himself to us through the Holy Spirit by the Church's advocacy of pro-life teachings in defense of the sanctity of all life.

The choice is therefore asking a mother to nurture that fetus until birth, and then if she chooses making the decision to allow for adoption. It is a temporary measure, but allows the fetus to live and therefore a pro-life decision. The Church needs to work to provide resources for these mothers to be able to minimize the difficulties that an unwanted pregnancy could cause unbearable grief, if an abortion had been chosen.

It is important that people realize that an unwanted pregnancy is not unlike other catastrophes people experience in their lives, as serious illnesses, cancer, loss of limbs, loss of jobs, homes, death, etc. Any events that disrupts people's lives for a period of time; however the length, do not require necessarily a permanent solution such as an abortion. Abortions, death and suicide is eternal, it cannot be reversed. It is why we encourage; "Choose Life" and we will be there to help you without condemnation.

It is unfortunate that zealots professing a position on ethical, religious, or moral issues gravitate to extremes in arguing their issues. These actions often extend to promoting intolerant utterances or committing physically abusive actions against others, who disagree with their positions. Our advocacy should be to treat others with love, dignity, and compassion so as to dissuade them from leaving their faith.

The time requires us to steward our resources of time and energy to evangelize and provide the resources necessary to promote viable alternatives to people who feel their only choice is an abortion. Those new alternatives for them must be so meaningful that they will choose life for their fetus. We cannot win a war against abortion by violence and intimidation; it must be by gentle persuasion that wins the hearts of the pro-choice movements into accepting alternatives to stop more deaths than the 55 million abortions that have already occurred in the United States and over a billion worldwide.

SHORTAGE OF PRIESTS AND NUNS

The consolidation of churches as a result of new membership from other congregation joining the Universal Catholic Church will require appropriate planning of resources and expenditures in order to eliminate overlapping duplicity in administration, properties, and liturgical functions.

Lower attendance even though membership may grow requires purging of registered non-active members, who do not attend on a regular basis, to determine active membership to restructure revenues and to establish balanced budgets. No longer should parishes continue to maintain edifices for the sake of traditions or personal preferences. The emphasis needs to be on the pastoral needs of the congregations, and its outward ecumenical evangelization rather than on a church facility.

Many of the non-Catholic congregations that have married clergy and possibly a family to sustain, have already dealt with the issues related to appropriate salaries, compensation and benefits. There is already a historical precedence so that we do not have to reinvent what is an effective system. This would have a major impact on the size of a congregation.

Building large elaborate edifices beyond the means of income levels of parishioners will no longer be allowed. In large metropolitan population centers, one church facility should have the capacity to meet the needs of parishioners within a reasonable distance to travel. No longer should catholic churches be within ten miles of each other, unless the facilities are maxed out based on current utilization. New facilities should only be built when economic realities dictate the more prudent course would be to replace aging, inadequate facilities or merging parishes. In non-urban areas smaller more functional facilities should be built. Evaluating aging structures, the elimination of underutilized churches, and restructuring diocesan needs in relationship to existing active working priest's assignments needs to be accomplished.

Priests within parishes should only be responsible for the liturgical and pastoral needs of their flock. Laity is more educated and knowledgeable of business affairs and should be assigned the primary responsibility for administrative functions of their parishes. In some cases, clustering of administrative staff should be providing those services for a singular parish cluster or for multiple regional clusters. Laity involvement in the church is highly recommended in helping to facilitate all the liturgical ceremonies and ministries.

Nuns, brothers, priests of various ecclesiastical congregations or associations should consider the merging of their resources, facilities, etc. in order to develop a stronger self-sustaining financially viable organization. Their physical facilities should provide the means of maintaining their membership identity without compromising their goals and reasons for existence.

The declining membership in old parishes are resulting in unsustainable financial burdens, sometimes with enormous debt, and aging structures. By maximizing economies of scale, closing old or underutilized facilities, parishes would be able to emphasize their continued spiritual mission and diminish their slow death by economic collapse. Larger revitalized parishes with the influx of new-dedicated parishioners will reenergize the truly active and dedicated parishioners, who devote themselves with their volunteering spirits.

The reason that these new non-Catholic mega churches are so successful is that they are not dealing with decaying old facilities for which elderly congregants do not want to let go because of familiarity, and their history of association with their church. These new mega-churches are making strides in being vibrant with active ministries that are appealing to new members. What people see with their old decaying facilities are diminished activities, and senior members. This is not very inviting for new young members.

Our churches must be organized and operated efficiently within their income resources, not operated out of continual economic crisis from which all resources and manpower is drained from the mission of evangelization, spiritual growth, and the reason for its existence.

CHAPTER 24

GANG OF FIVE" DISBAND

Cardinal Rossini meets with the other four Cardinals secretly and tells them it's time to disband, as truly this Pope has the blessing of God, and that all their attempts at stopping him have failed. He has also made notice that a number of Cardinals and other high-ranking church members, who have been rumored to belong to the Illuminati, have recently disappeared and their membership has been decimated. "This is beyond human control. We have no choice, but to submit our resignations immediately and seek redemption. We will not speak of this anymore." The other four Cardinals leave the room without speaking.

CHAPTER 25

CONCLAVE BEGINS

Vatican City appears to be in military lockdown. Security is unprecedented in order to thwart any actions by terrorist that might try to disrupt the Conclave from happening. Everyone has been given electronic security badges with their pictures and fingerprints in order to avoid stealing of credentials or other security breaches within the city. All vehicles except military, police and ambulance personnel have also gone through intense security screening are allowed. Vendors bringing supplies for the attendees are stopped at security gates were their merchandise are screened for explosives or tainted foods before being transferred onto a military truck for travel within the city. Military aircraft are keeping the area protected from assaults.

The Conclave will be held in St. Peter's Basilica in order to provide greater privacy and security for attendees. All manner of conveniences have been brought into the Basilica to accommodate all the various cultures and languages of its members. Supporting staff from the United Nations have been secured in order to provide a smooth progress for impending meetings. Additional temporary housing needs have been brought in to allow its members to stay within the security confines of Vatican City. A perimeter building along the security gate has also been set up to handle all press briefings for the worldwide news agencies gathered to bring coverage of the event. However all external news agencies are prohibited within the perimeter, except for the Vatican TV and Radio staff. They will provide the electronic feeds for distribution to outside news outlets.

The Conclave is expected to last a minimum of one to two years before its work is anticipated to be concluded. However, as major agreements on various doctrines, policies and governing guidelines are completed, they will be released as they occur. Until then, the final documents provided by the College of Cardinals for the Conclave members to review, amend if necessary and finally approve will be the interim operating documents and regulations for the Universal Catholic Church.

Pope John XXIV has also issued an order that all Cardinals and Bishops, including the Pope himself will have a mandatory retirement at 75 years of age. Further, should five members from the College of Cardinals deem appropriate, that they can request a medical and psychological exam of the Pope or any prelate to determine their continued ability to maintain their position within the Church. The Pope has expressed that no longer will the

Pontiff be controlled by caretakers of subordinates who usurp the responsibilities of a Pope, Cardinal or Bishop. The governance of the church is too important to allow a prelate from properly resigning their positions when they are no longer able to function in that capacity. A three member panel of renowned medical specialists will be assigned the task of completing such an evaluation. A simple majority opinion of the specialists will determine whether a prelate is to continue or be removed for medical reasons.

Pope John XXIV has entered the Basilica to start the Conclave with a Mass of Thanksgiving that this day has arrived. Many of the attendees who have not completed the prerequisites for priestly ordination and acceptance of the Pope as the Head of the Universal Catholic Church will be performed at the most opportune time during this Conclave.

Pope John XXIV intones the beginning of the Mass. "My dear brothers and sisters, we are gathered here today to advance the next step in our journey to bring about the major work of the Conclave to secure the theological doctrines, regulations, and operational guidelines that will allow us to operate as the Universal Catholic Church. This new endeavor unites all Christians around the world into Christ's church on this earth, in preparation for our journey to Him and our Heavenly Father in Heaven." And the mass continues.

After this liturgical celebration, Pope John XXIV returns to his papal apartment and looks at his constant companion Peter, his fond puppy, and says, "Let's go for a walk in the garden. We have a lot to consider about what comes next!"

THE END

BIBLIOGRAPHY

1 http://www.usccb.org/bible/matthew/19:12 /permission
Scripture texts in this work are taken from the New American Bible, revised edition © 2010, 1991 1986, 1970 Confraternity of Christian Doctrine, Washington, D.C. and are used by permission by the copyright owner. All Rights Reserved. No part of the New American Bible may be reproduced in any form without permission in writing from the copyright owner.

2 *"Catholic Controversies" American Decades. 2001. Encylopedia.com 2 Mar. 2013*
"Republished with permission of "Catholic Controversies" Catholic Answers Copyrighted C 1996-2013. Permission conveyed through Copyright Clearance Center, Inc.

3 http://en.wikipedia.org/wiki/List_of_stadiums_by_capacity
Creative Commons Attribution-Share Alike 3.0 Unported License

(//Creativecommons.org/licenses/by-sa/3.0/) (CC BY-SA"), and GNU Free

Documentation License (//www.gnu.org/copyleft/fdl.html) ("GFDL") (unversioned, with no invariant sections, front-cover texts, or back cover texts).

4 http://usccb.org/bible/matthew/19/permission/
Scripture texts in this work are taken from the New American Bible, revised edition © 2010, 1991 1986, 1970 Confraternity of

Christian Doctrine, Washington, D.C. and are used by permission by the copyright owner. All Rights Reserved. No part of the New American Bible may be reproduced in any form without permission in writing from the copyright owner.

6 *THE HOPE OF ETERNAL LIFE LUTHERANS AND CATHOLICS IN DIALOGUE XI*

Common Statement of the Eleventh Round of the U.S. Lutheran-Catholic Dialogue.

Edited by Lowell G. Almen and Richard J. Sklba, Lutheran University Press,

Minneapolis, Minnesota

THE HOPE OF ETERNAL LIFE Lutherans and Catholics in Dialogue XI

The document, The Hope of Eternal Life, was developed as a resource by the Committee for Ecumenical and Interreligious Affairs of the United States Conference of Catholic Bishops

(USCCB) and the Ecumenical and Inter-Religious Relations section of the

Evangelical Lutheran Church in America (ELCA). It was reviewed by Archbishop

Wilton D. Gregory, chair of the USCCB Committee for Ecumenical and Interreligious Affairs, and Presiding Bishop Mark S. Hanson of the ELCA, and it has been authorized for publication by the undersigned.

Msgr. David Malloy, General Secretary, USCCB

The Rev. Donald J. McCoid, Ecumenical Executive, ELCA

7 http://en.wikipedia.org/wiki/Penitent_Thief

8 *"Catholic Controversies" American Decades. 2001. Encylopedia.com 2 Mar. 2013*
"Republished with permission of ["Catholic Controversies" Catholic Answers Copyrighted C 1996-2013. Permission conveyed through Copyright Clearance Center, Inc.

9 http://www.usccb.org/bible/matthew/22/permission
Scripture texts in this work are taken from the New American Bible, revised edition © 2010, 1991 1986, 1970 Confraternity of Christian Doctrine, Washington, D.C. and are used by permission by the copyright owner. All Rights Reserved. No part of the New American Bible may be reproduced in any form without permission in writing from the copyright owner.

10 *"Catholic Controversies" American Decades. 2001. Encylopedia.com 2 Mar. 2013*
"Republished with permission of ["Catholic Controversies" Catholic Answers Copyrighted C 1996-2013. Permission conveyed through Copyright Clearance Center, Inc.

11 http://www.usccb.org/bible/matthew/22/permission
Scripture texts in this work are taken from the New American Bible, revised edition © 2010, 1991 1986, 1970 Confraternity of

12 *"Catholic Controversies" American Decades. 2001. Encylopedia.com 2 Mar. 2013*
"Republished with permission of ["Catholic Controversies" Catholic Answers Copyrighted C 1996-2013. Permission conveyed through Copyright Clearance Center, Inc. Author: Donald A Michaud